AVI

CAPTAIN GREY

SCHOLASTIC INC.
New York   Toronto   London   Auckland   Sydney
Mexico City   New Delhi   Hong Kong

D0623273

FOR JOAN

ISBN 0-439-28307-8

12 11 10 9 8 7 6   6/0

Printed in the U.S.A.   40

First Scholastic printing, February 2001

Contents

CHAPTER ONE · *Something of my early life and how I came to be captured* ·

MY SISTER WAS BORN in the City of Philadelphia, as I was, she in the year 1770, I in 1772. She was named Cathleen, while I am called Kevin. Our mother having died when I was born, I do not remember her at all. Our father, a carpenter by trade, had fled Ireland for America carrying no tools but his hatred of the English, who, he said, "broke my heart, but never my soul."

When the War of Independence took firm hold on American patriots, our father, who knew no higher duty than to fight his ancient enemy, left my sister and me in the protection of our mother's cousin, a Mrs. Barry.

Mrs. Barry was a good woman; she housed us and taught us our letters. But being also a good woman of business, she was more concerned with her millinery shop than with her poor and always hungry relations. As a result, my sister and I, rejected by other children as riffraff, clung together and did mostly as we wished. This meant wandering off into the not distant forests where we played the hours away. Our pleasure, such as it was, was to live more like Indians than dwellers of the city, creating habits and skills that brought blessings, as you will see.

When the war was over, our father, whom we had not heard from or seen for seven years, came back to claim us. That it was our father there was no doubt, though it was he more in body than in mind. For seven years he had fought for the cause of Liberty, but it had, at last, cost him his soul. Without reducing his enduring hatred of all things English, he informed the world that the English Parliament had its equal only in the halls of American government. "The snake in Eden," he proclaimed, "was but the first politician." He wished to have no more contacts with governments, or as it turned out, with any society.

Having so stated his mind and asserted his claim to us, he announced that we were to find peace in the southern wilderness of New Jersey. There was nothing my sister or I could do. Nor did the pleas, not overly forceful, by our mother's cousin, that a girl of thirteen and a boy of eleven were not fit for such a living have much success. Our father, denouncing all tyrants save himself, made his word law.

So it came to be that in July of 1783, with nothing more than packs upon our backs, we boarded a ferry, and after crossing the Delaware, headed due east. Very quickly we were made small by the great green and quiet forests of southern New Jersey.

I do not know exactly how long we tramped, but it was for many days. Father, we had come to see, was completely mad. No sooner did he aim for one direction than he would change course and pursue yet another place. And while it is true that he led us, it was in reality my sister's Indian arts that allowed us to survive. Not that father noticed. His mind traveled other worlds. Just where he was going we had not the slightest idea, other than his repeated hope that there existed a place without benefit of government. Such hopes led us directly into calamity.

My sister and I had made the camp at the bottom of a little dell. Having secured the site, caught some squirrels, gathered some food, and lighted a fire, we sat and watched father become progressively more removed from us. He did no more than sit and stir the thoughts within his head.

For three days we stayed in that place, wondering whether or not we were ever again going to meet with human company. The rising wisp of smoke from our little fire seemed the very unraveling of our lives. Indeed, my sister began to consider what could be done to save us. For one thing was clear: the man who called himself our father was leading us to destruction.

But on the third day, while my sister and I sat, as usual, at some distance from our father, speaking in low tones about what we should do, we heard the sudden loud report of a pistol, so close and so shattering of the silence to which we had grown accustomed that we were thrown into a state of frozen terror.

This was just as well, for in an instant we saw that we were surrounded by a group of men. To have come upon anyone in so deep a pocket of eternity as this would have been startling, but to encounter men such as these was horrifying, as if we had stumbled into the mouth of hell.

The men were bedecked in a mixture of uniforms such as I had never seen, costumes of every color, order, and nation, rather like a company of players in which every actor was performing in a different play. The gay colors of their dress contrasted with faces stamped with fierce anger; no light of love or kindness shone in any eye I saw. They were armed with swords, pistols, cutlasses, and muskets. If we had been an invading army, they could not have met us with greater force.

One man stood out in front of the gang. A man, as I came to know him, who went by the name of Captain Grey. He was their leader, but he was not a big man. Compared to the others he seemed almost small. Indeed, his thin, pale face gave him a wasted look; but the hatred emblazoned upon his eyes, unwavering and instantly understood, was aflame with life.

He wore breeches and boots of a simple cut, and he alone among the men wore a shirt of plain linen, which gave him a distinctive look. Clean shaven, hair neatly tied, he held a sword in his hand. Round his middle he had wrapped a sash into which he had placed two fine pistols. He rather struck me as a gentleman.

"Who are you?" he demanded of father in a voice as hard and as tight as a nail.

Father, who seemed to have noticed nothing, remained where he was, seated on the ground as though his brain had turned to pudding. It was my sister who answered.

"We are wandering, sir," she said.

"What brings you to this place?" Captain Grey demanded.

"My father leads us," answered my sister again, indicating where he sat on the ground.

The captain looked down and saw the distant expression on father's face. "What's the matter with him?" he wanted to know.

To which I replied with youthful honesty, "He is mad."

The captain considered this for a moment, then strode over to father, kicking him cruelly upon the leg. Only then did father look up.

"Get up," the captain ordered.

"I get up for no man, king or president-general," replied father, in the absurd style to which he gave vent to his notions.

To this reply the captain reached down, and catching

father by the scruff of his shirt, hauled him to his feet as if he were a kitten.

"You'll stand when I speak to you," he said.

Father, for the first time, attempted to resist, though all he had left was his voice. He used that to its full measure, screaming insults at the man. To this abuse the captain replied with a backhanded blow to father's face. The shock of it quieted him instantly. He took to staring about, as if he had only now perceived that we were very much at the mercy of those who had surprised us.

"Now, then," said the captain, turning back to Cathleen, but not releasing father, "where do you come from?"

"Philadelphia," she replied.

"The great capital of the Republic," said the captain sarcastically. "May it rot. Where were you going?"

"I told you, sir, we were wandering."

The captain considered this direct answer, and under the eyes of his men seemed unsure what to do about it. "Are there any more of you?" he wanted to know, still dangling father.

"Just us," I said.

"Good," said the captain. "Then you can come along and be of service to my government for a time."

What he meant by this I had no idea. But it meant, alas, everything to father. The word "government" was to him like a spark to a bomb. With a shout of "Political beasts!" he—though still held by the captain—made a desperate grab for one of the pistols in his tormentor's sash. He managed to get hold of the handle but could not pull it out. This action, however, set the rest of the men to howling. The captain, feeling himself attacked, instantly dropped father on the ground and ran him through with his sword as if he were no more than an animal. Father died at once.

My sister and I stood witness to this dreadful scene, horrified. But it was my sister, as usual, who recovered her wits first. Snatching me by the hand, she tried to dash into the woods. Too late! The other men, with dreadful oaths, closed in around us.

Listening to my sister's cries, I found myself pulled away from her, while the captain screamed, "Secure them! Secure them!"

I attempted to resist but was surrounded by men of far greater weight and height than I. Knocked to the ground, I cried out to my sister. In answer I heard shouts, pistol shots, and screams—my sister's screams I was mortally certain.

In a matter of seconds—it was all the time required— silence returned. The captain hauled me up by my hair even as a rope was flung about me, binding my arms. I looked wildly about for Cathleen. She was nowhere to be seen.

Father's death, my sister's disappearance, my own captivity: it all happened within the space of moments. It is hardly to be wondered that I fainted.

CHAPTER TWO · *My first hours with my captors* ·

WHEN I REGAINED MY SENSES we had left the place where I had been captured. I had enough wit to look about me for my sister. Not seeing her anywhere, I was forced to the conclusion that I was leaving the last of my family behind me on a bloody ground. It is only honest to confess that while I felt the death of our father keenly, it was the loss of my sister that gave me the greatest pain, a pain mixed with fear brought about by the awful realization that I was now alone in the world.

Firmly held, half walking, or rather stumbling, half carried, I was marched by the party of men along paths that only their eyes could detect. I am not certain how far we went; it could not have been more than a few miles. But the farther we proceeded, the more aware I became of a distant, steady roar. Puzzled as to what made the sound, which increased the more we walked, I suddenly came, to my total surprise, upon the ocean shore. We had come far indeed with our father! Clear across New Jersey, to the very verge of the Atlantic Ocean.

The way we took led us along a little bluff that looked over an expanse of beach down to the water itself, which was a small bay. Set back from the beach, but not yet in the woods, appeared what looked like a village, a series of huts such as children might build with sticks. These huts, though not overly large, were built of timbers and boards. One of them was two stories in height, with a pitched roof and a high tower. These crude buildings were set about like a town, with narrow streets running between them, even with a common, open area in their midst. It was somehow like a toy village.

There was nothing childlike about those waiting for us, however. Twenty men had surprised us in the woods. On the beach in front of the huts stood perhaps forty more men, all heavily armed, dressed in the same odd mixture of uniforms that my captors wore. Clearly ready to strike at anything that touched them close, they appeared startled when it became certain that I was the only prisoner. We marched right into their midst, the men moving away to let us pass as the captain led the way. Though all eyes were on me, no one said a word, but I could feel their anger like a heavy heat. I almost felt thankful for the protection of those who were holding me so tightly.

We headed directly toward the largest structure, the one with the tower and the pitched roof. We reached this house—for so I took it to be—and some of the men, led by Captain Grey, entered. Straightaway I was led up some narrow steps, thrust into a room, and heard the door being shut behind me. Alone, I lay on the floor and cried a great deal. Finally I dropped into an exhausted sleep.

I remember that when I awoke I felt some confusion as to where I was. It was dark there under the roof with no windows. The smell of salt water, pitch, and tar gave me a fleeting impression that I was at sea. The only light pointed up from between the floor boards.

Insufficient as it was, this light allowed me to see that I had been placed in a sort of attic room fashioned atop the house. The ceiling was unfinished and rough, made from irregular slabs of wood. It was a dismal, close space; I could see instantly that there was no getting out of it. I was a prisoner, and as alone as any Robinson Crusoe.

There was nothing for me to do but to sit and think about my situation. But I could not. I did not know who these men in the strange uniforms were, or why they had taken me, or what they intended to do with me. I could do nothing but wait.

After a time I began to hear murmuring voices below,

voices that increased in volume though I could make out nothing distinct. Recalling that I had been pushed up a flight of steps, I made my way down as quietly as I could until I came up against the door. I recognized the captain's voice instantly. His anger, which he had wrapped about himself like a shroud, gave him a thin, sharp voice.

"No one," I heard him say, "will find their bodies. I want no more talk of that. It's done, and well done too."

"All right," came another voice. "Then what's to be done with the boy?"

"We should have left him with the others," said someone.

"He's a better fighter than the rest of you," I heard the captain say, much to my surprise. "How many of you did it require to take him?" Nobody answering, he continued. "Then I say he's worth something. I propose to educate him properly."

"Educate him!" cried a voice. "Listen to the gentleman talk!"

"He makes it dangerous for us," said another.

"A noose around our necks," agreed yet someone else.

For a moment no one said anything. They were waiting, obviously, for the captain to make up his mind.

"Bring him out here," the captain said at last. "I'll see what I can make of him. But mind, hold him fast."

Startled, I hastened up the steps and lay down on the floor pretending I was asleep, for I did not want them to know I had been listening to their conversation.

Feeling a boot against my ribs, I sat up as if I had just woken. At once, two pairs of hands were laid upon me and I was bumped and shoved down the steps.

When I entered the room there were four men with the Captain. They stared hard at me, and though I was truly frightened, I was determined not to let them bully me anew.

"What's your name?" Captain Grey demanded.

"Kevin."

"The rest of it."

"Cartwright."

"What were you doing out there, wandering about?"

"My father was leading us."

"He was a fool."

"He was honest," I returned, as much to my own surprise as his. But he seemed to take it only as a fine show of bravado, and allowed it as such.

"You'll have to make your own way now," he said after a moment. "Join with us, and we'll let you be."

"What has happened to my sister?" I asked.

"Forget her," he replied.

"I shan't!" I cried, making a sudden, foolish effort to break for the doorway. It was a wasted journey. At once all hands were upon me, and for my pains I was struck down and held roughly, though not before I managed to kick one or two of them.

"You are at least a fighter," said the captain with as much of a smile as he could manage when I was hauled to my feet again. "Do you like fighting?" he asked.

"I hate it," I returned, for I did from the bottom of my heart.

"For one who hates it, you do it well," he said. "What do you expect to do for yourself! You are alone. You are at our mercy, are you not? What shall you do?"

"I shall find a way to get free."

"Free!" he shouted. "You are here, with us now. You can forget about your father and your sister, or anybody else you may have known. You belong to no nation but this nation. Put him back where he was and don't feed him. Tomorrow we shall talk again about freedom!"

There was no fight in me. I was swept up and pushed onto the steps. The door was slammed shut, the bolt drawn. Once more I was left alone with nothing to feed upon but my own thoughts.

Thus passed the first day of my captivity.

CHAPTER THREE · *In which Captain Grey breaks my will* ·

THOUGHTS WERE INDEED all that I had with which to content myself. Ever true to his word, Captain Grey sent not so much as a bit of bread or a hand of water to me.

The only thing that concerned me, other than food, was the thought of escape. That alone, I was sure, was my salvation. I even allowed myself the hope that perhaps my sister was not dead but hiding in the woods, waiting for me to appear. But to go down through the captain's room would have meant instant destruction. That left only the roof.

The attic light was poor, yet not so poor (it now being day) that I could not see that the roof, irregularly made, might have a weak point. But the roof was so steeply pitched that I could reach only a few sections, those that were close to the walls. I walked about and sought out some spot, some chink where light came through, which would suggest a possible weak spot.

This examination of the roof took a long time; while those places I could reach were few, I examined each with the greatest care. In time my patience was rewarded. I came upon a promising bit that I could manage by standing on my toes. At once I attempted to enlarge it.

It was slow work, for it was very tiring to stand with my hands over my head for so long. Moreover, the longer I worked, the hungrier I became: food was never far from my thoughts. At one point, while I was working, the door below opened.

"Come down," was the demand.

Obeying the order, I was met by two men who had been among the ambush party. The first thing they made me do was dress in one of their strange mix of uniforms. Then they ordered me to walk before them out of the house and into the woods. I had no idea where they were taking me or why. One moment I feared for my life, for they were heavily armed. The next, I thought they might be setting me free.

We walked until we reached a small clearing. There I met with a dreadful sight; side by side were two grave mounds.

"Your father lies here," said one, pointing to the ground.

But I sank upon my knees before the other mound,

the one that covered my sister. They had the mercy to let me cry out my last hope there, then led me back to the house and my attic prison.

Driven by a now desperate desire to escape, I instantly returned to my labors on the roof, working as long as I was able. From time to time I became dizzy with tiredness, the awkward position, and hunger. Sometimes I slept. All in all, I never got the hole any bigger than large enough to thrust my hand through. At last I had to admit that it was useless.

It was while sinking into a state of despair that I was again called down with a sharp, "You're wanted."

Thinking that I had little to lose, and after all, eager for any company, I did not hesitate. I was met below by Captain Grey and three others. Food had been laid out on a table before them. To my eyes, and in my state, it looked a great feast.

I must have shown this on my face, for after looking at me for a while, the captain laughed. "Hungry then?" he asked.

"You've kept me hungry," I returned.

"Very well," he said, in his sarcastic way, so that I could not tell what he really meant, "you may come here and help yourself."

Hardly wanting a second invitation, I took an eager step forward, only to be held back by someone I had not noticed who had come up behind me. I was so angry I closed my eyes. I did not even want to look at the captain.

"Now, Master Kevin," said he, "your Philadelphia

manners notwithstanding, you may help yourself if you but agree to one thing. And that is that you allow yourself to be ruled by me, and stand ready to serve in our enterprise, letting such misfortunes as may have occurred be forgotten and not spoken of again."

"And if I do not?" I replied.

He shrugged. "You are free to starve yourself to death."

"I want you to let me go," I said boldly.

"Never," he said simply. Without further ado, he began to eat, inviting the others with him to do the same.

When they were done he repeated his offer, but somehow, I hardly know how, I still refused. For my nobility I was removed to the attic where I found myself, if possible, much worse for their torture. But my passion for freedom was renewed. Once more I returned to work on the hole in the roof.

It was of little use. The more I worked, the less I accomplished, reflecting both upon the toughness of the wood and the weakness of my arms. With greater and greater frequency I found myself in need of rest.

While I was resting directly below the hole and staring up at it, I began to fancy that it was growing larger and that I was beginning to sprout wings on my back. This dream went on at such length that I was beginning to enjoy the pleasure of flight when I was startled by the appearance of an eye that was looking down through the hole at me.

I shook my head; I even hit it with my hand to pry the nonsense away. But when I looked again the eye was still observing me. I saw now that it belonged to a bird, blue-grey in color and with a spread of soft red upon its breast—a common passenger pigeon.

The pigeon seemed to be as fascinated by me as I was by it; it kept staring at me, turning its head this way and that as if taking my measure. Outside, looking in, it seemed to me the very emblem of my desire for freedom, so close to my fantasy of escape that I felt a great surge of friendship for the bird.

Pursing my lips, I tried to imitate its call.

At this the bird poked its head down into the hole to get a better look at me.

Knowing that passenger pigeons show little fear of people, and are easily tamed (I had caught many of them in my rambles through the woods at home), I had a passionate desire to grab it. So I continued to call.

Closer and closer down through the hole the bird edged, while just as slowly I began to creep toward it, my hands extended for a snatch.

Suddenly, with a bang, the doorway to the attic burst open and someone called, "Come down!"

Startled, the bird pulled back. I could see its fluttering wings as it beat its way into the air.

It was a cruel moment for me. The pigeon had been a friend, a poor one to be sure, but a friend of my own. Now it too was lost to me by my tormentors. I was quite prepared to agree to any of their demands.

"Are you coming?" insisted the voice.

Slowly, I made my way down.

How many hours had passed since the last time I had

been called I was not sure, but once again food was spread before the captain and a few of his men. He was quite prepared to play out the entire scene once more.

That time I knew I was defeated even before he spoke. For while nothing would equal my hatred of him, I knew he would dash my resistance, simply because I had so little of it left.

"Well, Master Freeman Kevin," he began in his taunting way. "How is it with you now?"

I said nothing.

"Have you lost your speech in solitude, sir?" he teased.

The others made a brave show of laughter, but I think they were uneasy at the game.

"I have been thinking," said the captain, "about your freedom up there all alone. I like your spirit. I do. I like it very much."

I did not have even the desire to lift my eyes.

"So," he continued, "I shall give you this final, free choice. I will spare you, boy, if you will step with me. I shall teach you what you need to know, and as long as you do as I say, you'll live as free as the rest. But mind," he quickly added, "strict orders. You're to do as I say."

I did not know whether to believe him or not, or even whether it mattered if I did.

"You are a free man," he boomed. "Make your *free* choice!"

I dove for the food. The captain's uproarious laughter was my welcome as I became a member of Captain Grey's crew. It was the third day of my captivity.

CHAPTER FOUR · *A Message* ·

I MADE A PIG OF MYSELF, but I was hungry, desperately hungry, and I felt as though I could not eat enough. The other men, along with Captain Grey, finished first, and having thoroughly amused themselves at my "free Philadelphia manners," as the captain called them, left me to my joys.

As I finished, a man came in to watch over me.

"Are you done, then?" he asked.

I nodded, fairly sick with too much food.

"As well you might, lad," he said, gathering up the things that had been left. But he paused in his work long enough to whisper: "Between you and me, lad, you put up a decent struggle. You can be sure about one thing, and that is that Captain Grey never loses any fight he sets himself to win."

I looked up at the man, and saw at once that he was not one of those who had taken us in the woods. This in itself made me look more kindly upon him. He was rather short and stocky, with a pale, deeply lined face and large hands that were ever in a state of twitching and clutching up into fists.

"Will he keep his word?" I asked, taking his manner as an offer of friendship.

"He will," the man replied. "But you've made a bargain yourself, don't you forget."

"What's to become of me?" I wanted to know.

"The captain makes the plans," he said, avoiding the question. "Now, if you're done, and I should think by heaven you should be, you're to go back to your room."

"Am I to stay there always?" I persisted.

"Now come along," he said with finality, "for that's what I've been told to do with you for now."

I got up slowly, even a little ill for all that I had stuffed inside myself. But, not knowing what might happen, I put a piece of bread into my pocket.

My foot on the first step, I stopped and turned to the man. "What's your name?" I asked.

"Benny," he replied.

"Do you always do what he tells you, Benny?"

"He's had the answers so far, lad, and that's the way of the world."

I went up the steps slowly, and once aloft, lay down. I was no longer hungry, but I was angry with myself at the bargain I had made, even a little ashamed. I knew it was the best I could have done, but I reminded myself that I was obliged to break my word if ever I had the opportunity. I had, after all, no real knowledge of what these men were about, or what they did, but I had little doubt that it would be evil. I was afraid they were pirates.

While I lay there thinking such thoughts to myself, planning complicated and absurd plots for my freedom, I heard a slight whirring noise. Looking up, I saw, to my great delight, that it was the pigeon perched upon the roof, looking down at me again through the hole. The pigeon, at least, was a friend.

I rather fancied that the bird took an interest in me, for it kept looking now this way and now that, even, for so I wanted to believe, nodding its sympathy at appropriate moments as I poured out my troubles in elaborate fashion. Nobody had forbidden me to speak to a pigeon!

Having sealed the bond of friendship with my tale of woe, I recalled that I had taken up a bit of bread from the table. My thought was that I could tempt the bird to make regular visits.

Standing up slowly, I took out a crumb, and with as much care as I could manage, moved my hand cautiously toward the hole, calling softly.

The bird, constantly cocking its head from side to

side, remained where it was until my hand reached the hole. After a careful examination of the morsel, its head darted forward, picking the crumb right out of my hand. Elated, I held up another bit, and the bird helped itself to yet another piece.

Then I had the notion that if I could draw the bird into the attic I could keep it there as company. With this in mind I moved my hand up again, but not so close to the hole as before. If the bird wanted more, it would have to move farther inside. And to my great satisfaction, it did.

I held up yet another piece, and to my infinite pleasure the bird jumped down through the hole, perched upon my hand, and began to feed itself to its utmost.

It was a common passenger pigeon, as fearless (or stupid) as any I had ever seen, but its interest in me made it seem a gay companion.

As the bird ate I talked to it some more. I asked its name, where it came from, what sort of business had brought it my way. Naturally, I received no answers but soft cooings; still, it was comforting talk to me.

Then I had another idea. I had heard of passenger pigeons being used to carry messages, and it came to me that I could use my bird to deliver a call for help. The moment this thought came to me I also saw how silly it was. To whom would a message be taken? Worse, if in some fashion the message came into the captain's hands, I would have broken my word and no doubt would forfeit my life.

Still, as the bird waddled clumsily about in search of more crumbs, I was swept up by the feeling that I must at least try. I resolved to do so.

What to write a message *on* was the first problem. I filled that need by taking up a corner of my shirt and ripping off a bit where it was already torn.

What to write a message *with* was the next dilemma. This took much longer to resolve, and while I tried to think of a way, I noticed, with some nervousness, that the bird took to fluttering about the attic in search of a way out. As it fluttered and bumped against the roof, it dropped a feather.

A quill pen, to be sure!

But no ink.

I searched wildly, for with every success I was more determined to send out something.

The attic room, as I said, had been made of old wooden beams. In looking at them I had noticed that they had been roughly cut, and in some places had been singed into a kind of smoothness.

Rejoicing, I pulled away some of the burned wood, crumbled it into my hand, spat on it, and stirred it with the point of my pen. Now I had ink!

Using the pigeon feather as my pen, I wrote out, in as small letters as I could, the message:

HELP ME

I twisted the strip of cloth around like a ribbon. Catching up the bird, I tied the cloth to one of its legs.

When I had made sure the knot was secure, I pushed the bird out of the hole.

Instantly it flew away. Where it would fly, I knew not—but all my hopes, and they were as vast as my message was small, were carried aloft.

CHAPTER FIVE · *My fourth day: in which I learn the dreadful business of Captain Grey* ·

I WOKE THE NEXT MORNING after a good sleep to a banging at the door and a rough voice which reminded me that I was still under sharp orders.

I ate in the kitchen of the house, a smoky place with walls black from a crude open fireplace that seeped smoke up to the rafters. While I was eating, Benny waited impatiently for me by the door.

When I was done he led me, not out of the building, but up a ladder into the tower atop the house, the curious structure that I had first beheld when I had arrived. We came up through the middle of the floor into a small, square room that provided an excellent view of the surrounding land and sea. Captain Grey was awaiting me.

The tower was so situated that he could see everything and everybody. Not a thing could happen without its being observed by the captain, and as I learned later, he spent a good deal of his time just watching.

Drawn up on the beach were a number of long rowing boats, while out in the bay itself was what looked like a floating platform. This platform had curious mounds at each of its four corners as well as a mound in its middle. The mounds were covered so I could not see just what they were.

When I arrived the captain was gazing out over the bay, which he continued to do for a while. Then he dismissed Benny with a curt order, telling me to stay.

"Did you have your breakfast, then?" was the first thing he said to me when we were alone.

"Yes, sir."

"Sleep well?"

"I did."

He grunted his satisfaction. "You see we lead a good life here. I shan't remind you of your bargain, but bargain it was, and bargain it will be."

He looked at me hard as he said these words, then, satisfied with the weight of his threat, he passed on to other things.

"This is *my* nation," he said, with a wave of his hand. "A nation truly free and independent. But you don't know how we do things, do you?"

I admitted I did not.

"Then I shall tell you," he said, "for you are now part of it." So saying, he drew out a scroll of paper and unrolled it; it proved to be a crude map of the bay before us.

"Here we are," he said, putting his finger to the place where they had constructed the cluster of huts. "That's the bay. Freeman's Bay, we call it. Not a prettier place on the whole coast of Jersey. I discovered it myself. On no map but mine, you see. It's deep, it's safe, and no one knows about it at all. What is more, no one else shall know of it. We take no prisoners, none at all."

"Now here you see," he said, referring to his map, "this spit of sand that runs before the mouth of the bay. Sand Island, the men call it, more sand than land, a resting spot for birds. That's all it's fit for.

"You see what it does, however: it hides the mouth of the bay. From out there," he said, gesturing toward the sea, "the bay can't be seen at all. What's more, that spit of sand hides our comings and goings. No one knows where we come from or, for that matter, where we go.

"Ships go up and down the coast. We spy them out, and when we choose, we get them. We take them and what they have, then we sink them down deep, without anyone knowing, if you please."

"With those little boats?" I asked, not sure if I should believe him.

"Do you see that?" he asked, pointing to the floating platform that lay in the bay. "When we get the signal from our man on that hill"—he pointed toward the high

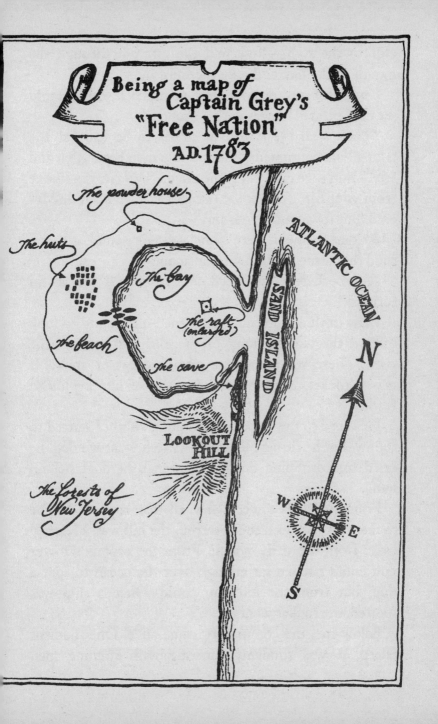

cliff to the right—"we pull the raft out through the mouth of the bay and take the ships by surprise."

I was still unsure how they managed it, but I could see how pleased he was with his scheme.

"There's all the world of riches to be had for the taking," he continued. "We are rich men here. Rich and free. Didn't we take you?" he cried. "We saw the smoke from your fire. At first we thought we had been discovered. But it was only you, and—"

At that moment there came a distant sound, a heavy thud that made the captain spin about.

"Look there!" he cried. "Now you'll see us in earnest!"

I saw nothing, not until he turned me around to look toward the highest point of the cliff that rose on the right. There, still rising, was a black streak of smoke. It was a rocket, leaving billowing smoke like a plumed feather.

He raced to the trapdoor and pulled it up. I started to follow, but he thrust me back. "Watch what we do," he cried, and dropping down, he banged the door behind him.

From the high tower I saw all that happened. The rocket that had been shot up from the hill was, I learned later, from the daily watch. From the captain's tower you could not see far enough over the ocean to spot a ship, but from the hill you could. Once a ship was spotted, the rocket went up.

Below me, the community came alive. One moment asleep, it was suddenly bursting with running men dressed in their strange uniforms, all racing toward the water's edge. There they leaped into the boats. No sooner was a boat full than it pulled from the shore.

Seven boats raced for the platform that rode so softly in the center of the bay. Reaching it, a number of men climbed aboard, which gave me a sense of how truly large it was. These men secured the platform to four of the rowboats with rope, and the boats began to pull the platform toward the mouth of the bay.

Another rocket streaked the sky, exploding with a thud. This rocket, I was later to learn, gave the direction the boats were to turn once they were out of the bay.

It was horrid work they pulled toward, but it was a marvel how it was done. I stood unable, and in truth unwilling, to turn away.

Within minutes the platform had been hauled to the mouth of the bay. There the boats turned left and were quickly lost to my sight.

All was silent and still. It was a long while before I heard anything, but when it came there was no mistaking the sound: the thudding of cannons rolled in from the sea, heavy and hot. The first cannonading was fierce, then it settled down to a rhythmic tattoo until it dropped away to nothing.

My first thought was that I had been saved. The cannonading could only mean—in my mind—the destruction of Captain Grey and his gang. At once I reached for the trapdoor and attempted to pull it up. My joy vanished when I realized that the captain had bolted it behind him when he left, leaving me a prisoner. I was thus in the curious situation of believing my enemies defeated but worried that my friends—whoever they were—would have no idea that I remained behind and alone.

There was nothing to do but wait.

I was in fact just daydreaming, thinking I know not what, when I heard, from a great distance, another round of cannon shot. What it meant was a mystery to me.

Then, after what seemed yet another hour or two, one of the longboats, in which Captain Grey himself was sitting, slipped into the bay. This was followed by two other boats, and quickly after, by the platform which was being towed by the remaining four boats.

The corners of the raft were no longer covered, and I could see plainly what had been hidden. Cannons! One stood at each corner of the raft. It was a floating battery.

My heart sank.

The cannon raft was again anchored in the center of the bay. Then commenced the unloading of a large pile from its deck, for the prize had been rich. Chests, barrels, and other goods were soon deposited on the beach, and from the beach they were transported to the captain's house. I looked in vain for prisoners. True to his word, the captain had returned with none.

I felt as if I had been forgotten. But already I had learned the primary rule of my new life: I could do nothing but wait for word from Captain Grey.

CHAPTER SIX · *The captain talks about my future* ·

It was dusk when I heard the trapdoor rattle, then saw it flung open. Benny thrust up his head, his face smeared with black. I saw that his clothes had been badly torn. Clearly, he had been in the very fist of the fight.

"The captain wants you," he said.

I followed him to the captain's room. Here all the spoils of their piracy had been heaped. I don't know what I expected them to have taken; I suppose gold or coinage. But there was none of that. Instead, it was a great heap of those things known as objects of wealth: to wit, frail dishes, fine books, silver candlesticks, good cloth and clothing, and so forth. I recall, in particular, a violin. There was even a portrait painting of some rich lady on the pile, her rosy-cheeked smile utterly absurd in that place.

Standing to one side of the room, I was able to observe the men of the gang lined up outside. At a call from the captain, they entered one by one. It was a kind of ceremony.

"Charles Conklin!" cried the captain, and a tall, round-shouldered man, who, like Benny, was much the worse for the day's activities came into the room.

"You did well today," said the captain in a voice loud enough for those outside to hear. "As a free member of this free nation, you may have that part," and he indicated what things might be taken away.

The men took them, too, even in their broken, blood-stained uniforms. They took them not in kindness, but grasped them in their hardened hands, as if to say, "These are mine. Touch them if you dare." They frightened me. As well they might: the man who took the violin crushed it before the day was done. Why? It played not well for him.

So it went, one man after another, until the pile of goods dwindled away. To my surprise, the captain took nothing for himself. When all was done, the captain dismissed Benny, ordering me alone to stay.

"Well, then," he said to me, "did you see how it works?"

"As much as I could," I replied.

"Very nicely done, is it not? She was only a small ship, but as you saw, she had a few pleasant things."

"What happened to the ship?" I asked.

He looked at me severely. "I see you don't ask what happened to your mates."

"They aren't my mates," I replied.

A moment of anger crossed his face, and just as quickly turned to a smile. "You have your toughness, you have. I suppose you've sworn yourself a revenge upon me. If you are what I think you are, you have. And more power to you," he added, with a nod.

"Why have you shown me all these things?" I wanted to know.

"It doesn't do for someone on the inside to be close to the captain," he said after a moment's thought. "You are from the outside. I need someone I can trust, someone I can raise up to a more perfect understanding of my ways." He looked at me. "Perhaps you will be captain here someday."

He must have seen the surprise on my face, for he added, "Doesn't that appeal to you?"

I was unable to give an answer. It seemed too astounding to me.

"I shall be your teacher," he went on. "This much I know: you are a fighter. How old are you?"

"Eleven years."

"If you struggle as much at this age, you'll do finer things yet. Your education has already begun. You will notice that I took nothing. All that I need is what I have here." He touched his head. "And if they take that, *they* have nothing."

There was not a word I could say to him.

"Have you eaten?" he asked.

"No, sir."

He called for Benny and commanded him to get me some food, after which I was to be sent to my room and locked up. I turned to follow Benny.

"Remember what I told you," he called.

For dinner I was given more than I had eaten at breakfast. Most of the food, if not all of it, had been taken from the ship they had sunk. I ate as much as I wanted, managing to hide some for my pigeon friend.

Once done, I returned to my room. I didn't need to be pushed, but mounted the steps and lay down on the floor, thinking of what the captain had said to me.

The thought that I was to be his particular friend was absurd to me, but I had no doubt that he meant every word. Not forgetting for a moment my resolve to have my freedom, I decided that the best action on my part would be to act in compliance with his wishes. For I realized that I would, in all probability, have but one opportunity to escape, and I had best make the most of it. With such thoughts tumbling through my brain, I fell asleep. And so passed my fourth day.

There is no telling how long I might have slept if I had not been awakened by a curious sound and a poking at my fingers. I was so startled that I leaped straight to my feet, only to be met by a great fluttering and squawking. The pigeon had come back, and remembering the crumbs I had offered before, it was pecking at my hand. My leap had frightened it so that it retreated to the other side of the room and now watched me carefully. I had to smile at my alarm. Even so, I worried least my friend, the only friend I had, should become fearful of me.

By the faint light of dawn I got down on my hands and knees and brought out the bit of food I had saved. Tearing off a piece, I threw it toward the bird.

The pigeon did not move, but stayed motionless. Then it strutted over to the bit of bread and pecked at it, first curiously, then quickly.

Throwing out some more crumbs, I edged closer. Soon I was near enough to catch the bird in my hand. I stroked its feathers, and as I had done before, told it all that had happened to me.

When I had finished my recital, I inquired, after the fashion of friends, about what the bird had been doing. I do not think I would have been surprised if I had received an answer.

Suddenly I remembered my message and looked to see if it was still on his leg. It was gone.

That my message was gone set me off on a new set of dreamlike questions. Had someone taken it? Who? If a person took it, why was there no message in return?

All this was foolish of me, of course, but you will understand that even the smallest hint that I was talking to someone—it had to be someone from within the community—was too real a desire for me to deal with other than as true hope.

I finally decided that the message *had* been received by someone unwilling to answer for fear of the captain.

This led me to the next obvious step—that I should write *another* message, equally cautious, without identifying myself.

Putting the bird down carefully, I wrote out a line as I had done before, with a rag, soot, spit, and feather. I wrote:

DID YOU RECEIVE MY MESSAGE?

As before, I tied the cloth to the bird's leg as securely as I could. I was fairly certain that if the bird had come back once, it would come again, at least as long as I had crumbs, and I wanted to be certain that the absence of the message was not an accident. Then I sent the bird off again through the hole in the roof.

My effort at communication done, I lay back on the floor, but instead of returning to sleep, I worked up mountains of fancies as to my future. Most of all I resolved to observe the men in the camp for some clue as to who had answered me. I was still musing in such a fashion when I heard a knock, and Benny's voice calling me for the day.

His call brought me back to my true world, but somehow I was no longer frightened. It was as if the bird, by allowing me contact with *somebody*, had given me new strength.

CHAPTER SEVEN · *My continuing education* ·

I HAD LEARNED the means by which they lived—plundering ships that passed along the coast—and now Captain Grey took an entire day, my fifth, to show me about his "nation," as he insisted upon calling it.

At each hut—it was hard to call them houses—he knocked on the crude door and begged admittance. To each man he introduced me as "Master Kevin" and asked if they "would be so good as to consider me a citizen in good standing." Each man in turn replied with solemn stiff salute. Captain Grey seemed to want them all to know that I stood under his particular protection.

The small buildings, all constructed of planks and beams, were crude enough from the outside. Inside, however, they were anything but simple. For each man's house was as gaudy and bedecked as his uniform, filled with the stolen stuff of his plundering. I saw paintings, cloth, books, dinnerware, and other objects of value. It was as if each man, though living alone in that strange place, lived the life of a duke.

As we went from house to house the Captain would tell me something about the man we were about to meet. Thus: "Here's James Pitman, gunner. A way with a gun as you might pay attention to." Or, "William Leider. A nasty sort, whom you will not want to cross. You jump when he tells you to."

Each man looked upon me as a curiosity, not saying a word, just staring at me as if to mark me for what I was, a quirk in the captain's ways. If any man questioned my existence then, I never heard it.

Of particular interest to me was their attitude toward the captain. They respected him, trusting him as their leader. Whatever fear they had of him—and fear there was—was secondary to their other feelings.

"May I ask you a question?" I said as we were moving from one place to another.

"You can ask."

"Why have you picked me? There must be others here who would have served you better." To this I added, in my outspoken way: "You must know what I think of you."

"Do I?" he said, his face blank of any emotion.

"I hate you," I said.

"Hate is a necessary thing," he replied blandly, moving on.

"Why don't you get your own children to do your work?" I called after him, smarting over his indifferent reply.

Instantly he wheeled about, shot out his arm, and with the full force of his strength struck me squarely upon my face, sending me, as much by surprise as by the force of his blow, sprawling backward on the ground.

I had not had such an easy life. The fact is, however, that I had never been struck with such anger in all my days. It ripped away any of the peace that I had allowed myself to feel with my new situation. I was hurt, and in pain; but it was nothing to the hurt I felt within. I burst into a flood of tears, more for shame than anything else. The image that loomed large in my mind was that of my sister. Oh, how I missed her!

"Get up!" the captain ordered.

I needed no second request; I rose, rubbing my face with a trembling hand.

"You may be as bold as you like," he said, "but confine yourself to this world, this time, and your future. There is nothing else that matters to you."

Refusing to say anything more, he continued on with his introductions, which were, if possible, even briefer than they had been before. When we had done we marched back to his own house; here he left me, without another word or look.

Right then, I could have fled. Indeed, I believe at that

moment I might have made good my escape. But I did not. What is more, standing there, I knew that escape was *not* my prime desire. Escape was too easy, too much just for myself. What I wanted was revenge.

From that moment my attitude toward the captain and his "nation" changed. For I was quick to understand that, in some fashion, I held something over him. Something about me, something I did not know, was important to him. If I learned what it was, I could work it to my advantage. So too, I knew I had to be careful, because as much as it was in my power to use that "something" against him, that something drove him to sudden violence.

I believe that my explanation of these thoughts takes longer to set down than it did for the entire idea to run through my head: in fact, it came to me whole, complete.

Thus fortified, I resolutely marched into the kitchen ready to demand what I wanted.

Benny appeared a few moments later. "What did you say to him?" he asked me right away.

I told him.

He shook his head. "It's not wise to question him that way."

I asked him why.

"He had a family of his own," said Benny.

"What happened to them?" I demanded.

"All dead."

"Why? How?" I insisted.

But Benny only shook his head.

"You're all just afraid of him," I said boldly.

"I am," agreed Benny, taking no offense. "He burns into you, make no mistake. He's well worth taking the fear of. It is not," he added, "as if you were a bird and can fly where you want." So saying, he left the room.

I went back to my room without being led, falling asleep that night wondering what had happened that had so touched the captain. And what did Benny mean by talking of birds? Was it *Benny* who had received my message? I was determined to find out.

But the next few days I was unable to find out a thing, at least not from the captain. It was Benny who waited on me. The captain, so I was informed, had taken to his tower and was not prepared to come down.

I tried to find out why, but learned only that it was the captain's pleasure to retreat to this place, where he remained, so it was suggested, days at a time, never once to show his face, his hatred, or his hidden past.

CHAPTER EIGHT · *The sixth day.*
Learning my new trade ·

CAPTAIN GREY DID NOT APPEAR for the better part of the week. Not that I was idle. Jacob Small had been cast as my tutor, and he spared no moments to instruct me.

Jacob Small was a man of ordinary size, but of such strength as I have never seen before or since. His arms were as round as a cannon, his chest a barrel, his face florid with his exertions. Yet his hands were small, almost delicate, and he moved with great dexterity. He was the chief gunner on the raft, the very hand to the captain's violent strategy.

"You're under my charge," he announced to me the day after I had challenged the captain. "You are to stay with me and do as I tell you. Aye, and learn it too. I answer to the captain, and you would be wise to do the same."

It was a brilliant, blue day. Overhead, thin streaks of clouds pointed like fingers of lace toward the north, but their very whiteness seemed to make the sky that much a deeper blue. The August sun made the beach vibrate with heat, yet a spirit of lightness was about. The bay itself was smooth, but as I stood at the water's edge, I could see the ocean breaking on the far side of Sand Island.

"Is it always so calm?" I asked him.

"Yes, and good for us, you see. The ships that go up and down the coast can't put on that much speed. But we can. And don't we do it right?" he asked, not caring if I replied or not. "But with September," he continued, "the big winds will come. Sooner perhaps. Hurricanes and gales. We shan't trouble ourselves then. Perhaps we shall be gone."

"Then you don't intend to stay here forever?" I asked, surprised.

"I shouldn't think so. Not here!" He led the way to a small boat, almost a cockle, it was so round and plump. I got in, while he pushed us off. Once afloat, he sat up front and with a small paddle sent us straight out to the center of the bay, toward the floating battery.

Carefully, with great skill, Jacob sent us against the platform. It had seemed large enough from the shore; close, it was no less than enormous. It was in fact really no more than a raft, a huge one, made of heavy boards attached to tree trunks, trunks so large they were not all submerged.

In the center of the raft, as I have already described, was a great square box, while at each corner, covered by canvas, were the cannons.

After thrusting me on board, Jacob came along himself. He took off the protective cloth from one of the cannons, each of which was attached to the deck of the raft underneath by block and tackle.

"Eighteen pounders," he announced.

They looked large enough to me to throw greater weight than that. "How far can they shoot?" I asked.

"More than a thousand feet, but we get much closer. That's when you do real damage."

"How close?"

He smiled. "You'll see soon enough."

"What's in there?" I asked, pointing to the large box in the middle.

"Charge and shot," he answered. "You want it as far away from the guns as possible. There's always a danger of explosion. One hard knock and it could blow up all of us. Not that we have to use that much. A few good rounds and it's done. The rest is hand to hand."

Urging me back into the cockle, he pushed off toward the mouth of the bay.

"Are we going out to the ocean?" I asked, for as we moved farther along, the waves, breaking over Sand Island, seemed bigger than I had thought them.

"Not if we want our lives, we won't."

Nonetheless, we kept moving toward the mouth of the bay, which made me nervous. But as we approached, though Jacob paddled as much as he had done before, the boat made no progress. We even seemed to be swept back.

"The tide," he informed me. "She pours in, she pours out. A river this way, then the other. We've come close to losing a cannon more than once. You couldn't pull against this tide if it were oxen hauling. In or out, it doesn't matter which way."

I watched, fascinated. The waters at the mouth of the bay did move like a river, churning, foaming, swirling in endless eddies and whirlpools. It required all of Jacob's skill to keep us in one place for even a few moments, until he managed to slip us off to one side. Then he sent us to the far side of the bay, toward the base of the lookout hill.

This high hill was different than I had imagined it to be from the shore. It really had two sides, one facing the sea. The land side sloped, and was thick with trees from top to bottom. The side that faced the sea was a sheer cliff of grey-black rock, broken only at the bottom by masses of boulders and broken stone.

"You have to go through the woods to reach the top," said Jacob. "It's not an easy climb, but you can do it. Seaside, there's no way up at all."

"Who's up there?" I asked, remembering the rocket that had been sent skyward as a signal.

"We take regular turns," said Jacob. "You can see a ship at twenty miles. I shall take you someday."

That said, he sent us off again to the center of the bay, then let the tide move us so that we shot back toward the beach at the foot of the settlement.

"What's that house over there?" I asked, pointing toward a smaller building set off from the rest of the dwellings, a house I had not noticed before.

"We keep the extra cannons there," Jacob replied. "Our powder and shot too. You can't ever be too careful with that stuff."

I continued the rest of the day with Jacob Small, during which time he laid out particulars of the "nation": how it was built, and with what effort. He told me that all the wood for construction came from the ship that had brought them to the spot.

"What happened to the ship?" I asked, for it came to me I had seen no sign of it.

"The captain had it torn apart," was his answer.

"Why?"

"He wants us here," the sailor replied evasively.

I thought he was hinting at something. "Do you care for the Captain?" I asked.

"He takes care of us all," he said after some consideration.

"And the men take him for their leader because of that?"

"I suppose," he answered briefly.

"And they are proud of what the captain has made of them?" I ventured.

"What were we before?" he said scornfully, spitting into the sand. "As much as that."

"You don't answer my questions," I told him.

"The only questions worth asking are the ones that have answers worth having," he returned. "And with that in your mind," he continued with an angry look, "I'll ask *you* a question. How long do you think you would last around here if it wasn't for his protection?"

"I can protect myself!" I said stoutly.

"I wouldn't try," he said. "We continue your lessons tomorrow," he suddenly added, then turned his back and left me.

After I had eaten, I went up to my attic place, where I found a bed of straw had been laid out, clearly meant for my sleeping. After lying upon the earth or a wooden floor for so long, I found it wonderfully soft. I fell asleep thinking, as I always did, of all that I had seen and heard.

My thoughts must have carried into a dream, for I recalled that the pigeon had not visited me that previous morning. This made me suddenly wake, and sitting up, I looked out of the hole in the roof, realizing that I had slept through most of the night. The greyness marked the dawn.

The sudden awakening chased away any thoughts of further sleep. I contented myself with lying back, hands beneath my head, concocting idle thoughts. It was while resting thus that I heard the unmistakable whirr of feathers and a gentle scratching noise. The pigeon had returned.

I waited, unmoving, not wanting to scare the bird away. Within moments I heard more scratching noises from the hole. Soon the bird was walking about my floor.

I cursed myself for forgetting to bring any bread, having to satisfy myself with holding out a bare hand and calling softly. The bird came over and gave a peck to my fingers. Instantly I clapped my other hand down and held it close. Feeling for its legs, I found a bit of cloth tied around one of them. It felt just like the bit I had put there.

Disappointed, I untied it, wanting to be sure that it was my own message returned. But once I had it in my hand, the problem was to read it. Peering down the steps I saw a thin sliver of light beneath the door. I crept down, untwisted the cloth, and looked to see if it was my message.

The first thing I made out was my own words:

DID YOU RECEIVE MY MESSAGE?

By some quirk of thought I turned the ribbon to the other side. My heart leaped. Somebody *had* written another line. Six days into my captivity, another human had answered with the words:

WHO ARE YOU?

CHAPTER NINE · *Some considerations about the message* ·

THE MESSAGE WAS ENOUGH to send me walking up and down my attic room until long past the brightening dawn.

The very thought that I was communicating with someone, somewhere, excited me. Still, there were other considerations: I had assumed that it was a friend, somebody who might help me escape. I made myself admit that it was quite possible that it was not a friend at all. Indeed, the fact that I had seen no other human aside from the men of Captain Grey's strange "nation" meant that there was every chance it was someone who would report my message to the captain. Jacob made it clear enough that I was not welcome. If it was a trap, and I got caught in it, I would be lost. I would have to be exceedingly careful in my reply. If my message was intercepted, I would have to find means to argue myself out of grave difficulties.

My first decision, then, was to continue the messages without revealing my name, indicating only that I was being held somewhere. I would see if that brought about a response that encouraged trust. Furthermore, I decided that I had to learn if any of the captain's men kept pigeons. If someone did, I would need to know more about him.

Having decided all that, I thought out a message that would be proper, striking upon the phrase: *Will you help me?* But before I had the time to write it out, there came a thumping on the door below.

"Up you come, lad! Past times. Past times!" It was Benny.

Fearful that he would come up and discover the pigeon who was now sleeping at the far end of the room, yet wanting to keep him until I could send the message, I grabbed a fist of straw from my bed and plugged the hole, then hurried down the steps.

"Is the captain out?" was the first thing I asked of Benny.

"Not a bit," he replied. "I told you, lad. He's not the one to send out messages. You're looking the wrong place if you're looking for that from him." So saying, he went to the kitchen.

I stood rooted to the spot, thinking of what he had

said. Was it really Benny who was my special friend? I wanted to think so. But before I could proceed any further, I was called outside to Jacob Small.

It was not the day it had been before: grey clouds were piling over the ocean, and I could feel a fresh, wet, salt wind coming in from offshore. So it proved. As the day progressed the weather turned harsher.

The change in weather, however, did not prevent Jacob from giving me my day's lesson, which for the most part consisted of teaching me how to use the oar.

It seemed perfectly easy when I watched him, but I proved totally inept when I did it myself. Jacob wasted no words at all, but let me know when I did it badly. This he did by setting us in the middle of the bay and insisting that I take us back to shore, while he sat back.

My first hour was spent driving us about in little circles. Jacob, for once, laughed. In his way he was very patient, but his method of teaching was short on explanation and long on expert demonstration, which I simply could not imitate.

The winds increased and the clouds built higher. We were being tossed in every direction, but he would not quit my lesson.

"Can't we go in?" I urged.

"Not till you've learned," he replied.

We therefore spent most of the day on the bay, and before we were done the waters were like a pot of boiling oatmeal, with a steady blessing of cold rain to comfort us.

"I'm tired," I pleaded.

"All the more reason to do it right," was his reply.

When he was at last content with my learning, he urged me toward shore. I managed this with the best of will if not the greatest skill.

"Well done," he called to me as we ran up against the beach.

We pulled the boat high up on the sand and turned it upside down so it would not fill with water, then turned for shelter.

Allowed to stand in front of Benny's fire, I was given food, some of which I managed to hide for my bird. Once done, I hurried to my room, finding the pigeon sitting on the straw. I sat down cross-legged and fed it from my hand, all the while stroking its feathers.

When the bird finished eating I gathered my writing materials. By the light of the door below, I wrote my message:

WILL YOU HELP ME?

I tied this message to the bird's leg, pulled the straw from the hole, and tried to push the pigeon out. Alas, it refused to go. I could hardly blame the bird; in fact, I was rather touched that it preferred to stay with me. Relenting, I let it down on the floor, stuffed the hole, then went to sleep.

I woke the next morning—the ninth day—to the same dismal storm beating about my head. Instantly I looked for the bird, and found it strutting impatiently up and down. If it had not done so before, I knew it would never fly away on that day.

As I was checking the message on its leg, the door below abruptly pulled open.

"Are you there?" cried a voice that I recognized at once as belonging to Captain Grey.

"Yes, sir," I replied.

Then, to my horror, I heard him come up. In an instant I grabbed the bird, and despite its resistance, pushed it through the hole in the roof. It was a gesture of panic. What was worse, when the captain came up he found me standing beneath the hole, looking up.

He observed me closely, as I did him. From me he cast his eyes around the room until he fixed on the hole. The water was dripping in.

"How long has that been there?" he demanded.

I shrugged as if to say it was always thus. Taking up a handful of straw, I stuffed the hole.

"I'll have someone patch it," he said.

The thought that my one means to the outside world might be blocked brought back my tongue. "It's not necessary, sir," I managed to say. "There's no windows here and it brings in air."

"Is that so?" He took it kindly, apparently not understanding what I was about. "I'll speak to someone about it. Did you sleep well?"

"Yes, sir."

He took one more look about, then turned to go. "Come with me," he ordered.

He led me to his own room and sat down behind his table. Benny had brought him his food, so I stood by while the captain ate. He did not offer me anything.

Only when he was done did he push the remains toward me, saying, "You can have what you want."

Having long lost any feelings about such treatment, I asked for no second invitation but did as much justice to the food as I could.

He watched me steadily.

"I understand you've begun to learn," he said at last.

"Yes, sir, Jacob Small tried to teach me."

"He says you work hard and will manage well."

"Thank you."

"Nobody has mistreated you, have they?" he asked.

"No, sir."

"That's the way it is here, fairness and justice, as does not exist anywhere else on this earth," he said.

"I wouldn't know, sir."

"You know it now," he snapped, then sank back into his own thoughts, coming back to me only after a while. "There is much to learn, and you had best do well at it. I shall want you to come with us as soon as you are ready. You are needed."

"I don't wish to go," I replied, standing.

"Why not?" he charged.

"It's a murderous business," I told him.

"You'll do as I tell you," he roared, ordering me to leave the room.

I was only too glad to go. I found Benny just outside the door. As he led me away, Benny mumbled, "It's your life when you challenge him that way."

But as I had decided some time ago, it was my life no matter what I did.

CHAPTER TEN · *My fourteenth day.*
I go to sea in battle ·

THE NEXT FEW DAYS were much the same, a constant education in seamanship and piracy, mostly at the hands of Jacob Small, but sometimes with others, rarer still with the captain himself. It was clear that I was meant to learn everything there was to be taught. There seemed no end of it. Once, when I made the casual remark to Jacob that I was but a poor swimmer, all else stopped until he taught me well.

As for my pigeon, it did not return. The hole in the roof had not yet been plugged; nonetheless, the bird failed to come back. I blamed myself for having thrust it out during the storm, and was certain that it had died, my message lost. Still, I managed to find the courage to ask Benny if any of the men kept pigeons.

"What do you want to know for?" he asked.

"I am curious," was the best I could manage, afraid to look at his eyes.

"No one has them," he replied. "Some live out on the rock side of the hill. That's all."

Disappointed, I let the matter drop. If he was not the one who answered, I was at a loss. It suggested someone outside the confines of the camp, but that I knew was impossible.

My training continued, though not so complete that I was allowed to go to sea. When the rocket went up, as it did once during the time, I was, to my great relief, locked in the captain's tower.

As for the captain himself, sometimes I saw him, as often I did not. There was no way to anticipate his moods, at one time friendly, almost fatherly, at other times mean, petty, and cruel. I could not sound him.

It was on the fourteenth day that I learned more. He had commanded me to join him in his tower; there, for hours, he said nothing but stared moodily out to sea. Then, his eyes still on some distant spot, he began to ask me questions about my father.

"Did you love him?" he asked.

"To the best that I could," I replied.

"Trust him?"

"Aye."

"And let him lead you as he would?"

"I did."

"Why?" he asked with contempt, still not looking at me. "Didn't he leave you? Didn't he treat you poorly?"

"He was the father I had," I said.

"He was worthless," continued the captain. "He spent his life fighting for others. The only fight worth fighting is for oneself."

I said nothing.

After a long moment, he suddenly said, "Could you look upon me as your father?"

"No," I said too quickly.

"Why not?"

"Because you make me stay here against my will."

"And if I let you go where you wanted, where would that be?"

"I would go home," I said.

Turning, he stared at me with a look I shall never forget, a look that expressed nothing but fear. "I will never let you go!" He was about to say something else, when abruptly, we heard a report, and springing about, we observed a rocket streak from the top of the hill.

"Now you shall be truly one of us," he said. "This time you will come!"

Kicking and pushing me before him, we tumbled down on the beach toward the boats, which were already beginning to leave the shore.

It was one of those balmy late-summer days, not a cloud in the sky, and the sun feeling hot no matter where one stood, a day on which the birds appeared to float more than fly, a day on which there were all kinds of excuses for doing nothing.

But the men who pulled on their oars were of no such mind. As the boats passed the cannon platform, ropes were flung out and some of the men, led by Jacob Small, leaped upon its deck and began to work the anchor. In moments, the floating battery was in tow.

Another rocket, shooting from the hill, exploded with a single report, telling us which direction to go out of the bay's mouth. The tide pouring out, we moved along with great speed, as though racing down a flowing river.

Throughout, Captain Grey, sitting tall, spyglass in hand, constantly shouted orders now to this boat, now to that, calling men by name, urging one faster, another slower, pointing out the slacker at the oars, praising the efforts of someone else. Seeing all, he let everybody know what he saw.

The men, dressed in their strange uniforms, were all armed with weapons: pistols, swords, muskets, and daggers of every kind, shape, and age, from the best Spanish steel to Jersey pig-iron bayonets. It was a crowd of clowns gone mad.

At the mouth of the bay I saw Sand Island close up for the first time. It was as it had been described, long, low, with nothing but sun and rock on its high spine. A few small trees, twisted and bent double, marked the futility of life there.

Once we shot out from behind the protection of the

island, smooth water was behind us. The ocean, rolling with high and heavy waves, marked a rhythm that was at one with my beating heart.

"There she is!" cried a voice before us. My eyes turned toward the open sea, then down the coast.

Captain Grey stood. "A merchant marine!" he cried. "Fat and slow!"

"What colors?" cried a man.

"French," replied the captain.

The men, as one, cheered.

The captain, scowling, gave his orders. "Custer! Porter! Take the lee!" Oars shifted. The battle plan was laid, as two of the longboats swept out to sea to out-flank any escape by the ship. The floating battery, pulled by the four longboats, continued its straight course toward the ship, rising and falling in the sea with ponderous motion. Because the wind tended to blow toward the coast at that point, it was difficult for ships to find their way out of the trap so carefully set.

The merchant ship, fully rigged, was a big one, but it was easy to see why she had been marked for attack. She was not fast, she was unarmed, and she was alone—the last was the most crucial point of all.

I had no idea how many crew she carried, but I quickly counted our force. There were seven boats in all, each with six men. Forty-two. There was the float-ing battery, three men to each cannon plus Jacob Small. I counted thirteen. By my reckoning we had set to sea with close to sixty men.

Slowly, the French ship approached, a wonder to my

eye. Her staysails had long been in view. Now the main topgallant staysail and the foresail billowed forward before her bloated hull, giving her the appearance of a mountain crowned with clouds gliding upon the sea and summer air, pushing forward without fear.

I have to admit that, horrible as it was, the scene contained a dreadful grace brilliant to observe. The man who had invented the system had an eye for beauty and for blood.

The pirates, plunging forward, worked in silence, the oars alone sounding as they cut the sea. From long experience, all knew what to do.

The hardest part was waiting for the floating battery to come up, for she was slower than the rest, and the captain's men had to be careful, lest they or their cannons be swept off by a sudden toss of waves. As it was, they kept the cannons covered, waiting to load only at the last possible moment, lest the powder get wet and misfire. The first shots were the crucial ones.

The French ship loomed larger and larger. As we drew closer we observed sailors begin to climb the riggings, arms waving, as if to greet us. It was their last opportunity to show their faith and trust in man.

Two of the longboats were now on the far side of the ship and were waiting for the cannons to creep closer, which they did, the four towing boats straining at the lines.

At last the crucial moment was reached.

The captain, suddenly standing erect, waved an arm. Someone on the ship actually waved back. But that was not the captain's intent. In more deadly response the four towing boats moved so that each corner of the raft was pulled in different ways, which had the effect of steadying the platform. At that point the canvas covers were swept off and the men leaped to load the guns. They could not have been twenty yards from the prancing ship, which still did not perceive its peril.

It was too late.

The first cannon shot forth with an enormous crash. The tightness of the lines, the steadiness of the platform, made the ball go true. I saw the fire from the cannon first, then the shot itself leap across the short water gap and slam against the ship's hull with a wrenching, splintering crush.

The mountain shivered.

I watched, amazed, as those who pulled the cannon raft swung about ninety degrees, presenting the second corner of the battery, and another cannon, to the ship. It too fired. Once more I saw the great ship shake.

And that is the way it went. Spun about like a turret, the raft presented one cannon after another, spitting load after load directly against the ship's lower hull. I could hear the terror and confusion on the ship's decks.

Twelve shots were fired. Twelve shots were true. Upon the twelfth explosion, the longboats that were not pulling the raft hurled themselves against the merchant ship from the other side. The men, dropping their oars, tied themselves to the ship, then sprang upon her with murderous intent.

Moments later, the towing boats joined them, but

from the other side. The captain's boat shot forward with such speed that I was sent flying from my seat to the bottom of the boat. Momentarily stunned, I scrambled up and saw the ship loom over us.

To my astonishment I was left alone, as members of the crew and the captain himself climbed up to the ship. I was too frightened to follow, but I could hear well enough what was happening: the shots, the scraping of blades, the screams.

The struggle did not take long. The ship, having been taken completely by surprise, crushed with cannonading, boarded instantly by men who cared little for what they faced, gave way quickly. A sudden silence told me the fight was over. All I heard was the licking, lapping breath of sea against the empty boats.

My legs weak, I climbed aboard the helpless ship. When my head cleared the railing, all that I feared lay visible before me.

That it was dreadful you might already have guessed, for no words of mine would be able to express the calculated cruelty of the whole affair. We had taken the ship by surprise, and the defense of her crew was but poor. Far from showing any mercy, Captain Grey and his men had made the crew suffer for their innocence. The only men alive on the deck were the captain's men. Those from the French ship's crew who had resisted lay dead upon the decks.

A quick glance informed me that at least twenty of the Frenchmen had died on deck. Those who remained alive were pushed below. The ship was rendered useless too: the deadeyes split, the rigging hung idle. The sails whipped and fluttered without command.

Under the captain's direction, his men were hauling up boxes and chests, anything of value. Goods were quickly piled in a great heap. Hardly pausing, the men began to load the stolen goods into the boats that lay below. The captain did not interfere other than to make sure that necessities were taken first—food and the like —after which the men were allowed to loot at will.

From beneath the deck I could hear cries, calls, and curses, but no one from the captain's "nation" paid them any mind. They went about their thievery in silence.

All things considered, not much was taken, though what was removed was surely the best cargo. Some twenty-five cases altogether, a small portion, no doubt, of what the ship held. Nonetheless, the captain and his men seemed satisfied.

Meanwhile, I wandered about the ship with no one paying attention to me, or saying a word. At one point I asked a man whose name I knew what was to become of the ship's crew, but he would not answer other than to point to the captain if I wanted my question answered. I did not dare ask him.

Once the loading was done, Captain Grey surveyed the deck for the last time, then gave sharp orders to re-board the longboats. I was struck with the sudden notion that I could hide someplace, so that when the ship sailed off, I would be able to go with it. I would gain my freedom and inform on the gang. But before I could find a place to hide, the captain, observing me, ordered me back into the boat. My heart sinking, I had no choice but to comply.

As we began to push away I turned to the captain. "What about the ship?" I asked.

"You'll see soon enough," he replied, calling on the boats to hurry.

I had no understanding what was to happen until, with a sudden, sickening dread, I discovered their intent. Jacob Small, once more on the floating battery, but now closer to the ship than before, began to load the guns.

"You'll not sink her!" I cried.

"Why not?" was his curt answer. "Doesn't France sink what ships she wills? Does not the United States?"

"But you've put men into the hold!"

"Let them appeal to their parliaments, kings, and congresses," he said. "They can form a committee and pass some laws."

Even as he spoke the first cannon went off. Such was its closeness and power that a gaping hole, splintered and torn, flowered upon the boat's hull. Water poured in.

The raft, slowly turning, began a casual bombardment. Above the smashing of the shot rose the cries, shrieks, and prayers of the men trapped on the doomed ship.

Their prayers went unanswered. As the captain called away his boats, the great merchant ship went over on her side, then slid beneath the waters, a great foaming bubble rolling over the spot as if to mark the place. Then the sea itself mercifully hid the shame. Soon there was nothing left of the dreadful act but the shrill cries of gulls who had joined us and, like scavengers without souls, plucked through the flotsam on the the waves.

"My nation over all others!" cried Captain Grey, holding aloft a cloth, much like a flag. It was white—pure white.

As the longboats pulled their way back to the secure bay, I lay on the bottom of the boat, sick in heart, soul, and body. Through it all, like something seen only dimly through a mist, was that fearful look the captain had turned on me just before we left.

What was it in me that he feared so—he who showed no mercy? It was utterly beyond my comprehension.

CHAPTER ELEVEN · *A friend* ·

WHEN WE RETURNED, the stolen goods were brought to the captain's house as before and divided among the men, the captain alone taking nothing. I was forced to sit and watch while it was done. I was so stunned that it was difficult for me to measure fully the inhumanity of what I had seen.

As I watched I could not help but see how unmoved the men were: not even the pleasure of victory gave them joy. They went about the division of stuffs with a coolness that only added to the terror. To me, they were men without hearts.

I renewed my vow of revenge, but that renewal was no longer directed only at Captain Grey but against the entire gang, his whole "nation." Nor did I feel that my revenge was only on my own behalf. I felt that I must act in the name of humanity. As far as I could see, their only desire was murder. They deserved the same.

The goods divided, the captain dismissed everyone but me. Once alone, he sat back in his great chair, triumphant.

"Well, then," he demanded, "what do you think of it?"

"What does it matter what I think?" I challenged.

"You will be the future," he replied. "My particular gift to the world." As I said nothing he coaxed, "Is it not a brave, clever plan?"

Still I would not speak.

"You don't care for it," he said scornfully. "You think it cruel. You think I have no feelings. You think I'm the Devil himself."

My silence gave my answer.

Leaning forward, he stared straight at me. "You are right. I have no feelings. I do only what is necessary."

"Why?" I finally managed to say.

He sat back, his eyes never leaving my face. "In this world all societies, all men, all governments, and all nations are but gangs of thieves who join together to plunder others. But *they*," he cried, "they pretend to do it for the glory of God and mankind. I alone do it because I like to. I am the only honest man in creation. I alone have the courage to act openly, honestly. Do you not think so?" he said with a sudden urgency.

"I do not know," I stammered.

"Then learn," he said wearily. With a wave of his hand he let me know that I was dismissed.

I went gladly, not to any food, but to my attic room, for I felt it was impossible to be with other people.

I climbed my steps slowly, thinking with sudden sickness what would have happened if I *had* hidden myself on the ship. Then I decided it would have perhaps been better if I had done so: better than to have been a living witness to all that had happened that day.

It took a long time for me to sleep, and it was a fitful sleep at that, the sound of screaming gulls constantly in my head. This calling began in time to lessen, change its pitch, till slowly but clearly it turned into a soft, sweet sound.

I woke with a start and looked about. Sure enough, my pigeon had returned. It took me a few moments to accept the fact that I was not dreaming but fully awake.

Holding out my hand, I coaxed the pigeon toward me. It approached with its slow, absurd gait. When it drew close I gathered it into my arms.

Only when my outpourings of feelings were done did I think to feel its leg. The pigeon *was* carrying a message. I hastily pulled it off, and with shaking hands unrolled it in the dim light. It had but one word, an answer to my question, "*Will you help me?*" The reply was:

YES

My heart seemed to give me sudden pain. *I had a*

friend. Someone was going to fight with me. I lay back on the straw as much relieved as if a whole army had been appointed to my needs. Instantly I gave myself over to the urgent task of trying to find my friend.

The easiest way to do it, I decided, was simply to ask. With such a purpose in mind I penned another message, one which read:

WHO ARE YOU?

As I had done before, I fastened the cloth to the bird's leg, and after feeding it some crumbs, sent it on its way through the hole in the roof. Once that task was complete, I lay back to the pleasant dreams and speculations as to who my secret friend might be. With what I took to be a sudden change in fortune, I fell asleep again with ease.

There was no message the following morning, my fifteenth day. I had not expected one. Indeed, I had come to the conclusion that whoever I was dealing with was being very careful, no more willing to expose himself than I. Accepting this, I was content to wait.

But the other parts of my life did not wait. Once more I was set to lessons. The new lessons, however, were of a more specific nature than rowing a boat, swimming, or the like: I was instructed in the arts of war.

Jacob Small cared for the cannons and the strange platform that bore them with meticulous concern. It was not just a matter of endlessly polishing them— which he did—but he constantly checked on their well-being, proud of their deadly work beyond anything.

He taught me with particular care how to uncover the guns and remove from the muzzle the plug, the *tampion*, that kept the guns dry at sea. He showed me how to bring up the gunpowder that he kept in measured cloth bags. These bags were made up in the powder house on shore, but a ready supply of them was always kept in the box built in the middle of the raft. The bag of powder was shoved down the gun barrel with a pole called the *rammer*.

The shot used was round; once rolled into the gun barrel it was kept in place by bits of old rag. Jacob himself primed the touchhole with just the right amount of powder. He then jammed in the fuse and lit it, using a hot coal from his coalbox. In this final step he used the greatest care, for the slightest mistake could blow them all up. He even kept the coalbox about his person as an extra precaution.

We did not, of course, shoot off the cannons inside the bay, but I had seen their deadly work. Once a cannon was ignited, its vent hole, which carried the fuse, shot up a plume of flame, the cannon shot off, and the whole machine leaped backward against its ropes. You had to keep out of the way lest your legs get smashed. Once a cannon was fired, it had to be cleaned and cooled, but as I explained before, it did not have to shoot many times.

The more I learned about such things, the more the men accepted me, beginning to see in me something of value, something less than a burden. Their trust increased.

Once I asked Jacob Small about the ship that had brought them all to the bay. "Did you come on purpose, then?" I wanted to know.

"So to speak," he allowed.

"From where?"

"From England, at first," he said, "but the ship was American. A transport ship, don't you see?" he added with a sidelong glance.

"All of you?" I asked, surprised. I knew that a transport ship was but another name for a prison ship. They had all been prisoners.

"No, not all," he replied carefully. "Not the captain."

"I don't understand," I said honestly. "Then who was he?"

"Captain of the ship," said Jacob, "then as now."

"An officer?" I cried, not really believing him. For if he had been captain, then the prisoners had been under his control: he was their jailer!

"Can't you see it?" said Jacob.

"I never saw his like before," I confessed. "What happened to the other officers?" I asked innocently.

"Too many questions," my friend replied, moving away so that I could not press him any further.

He had said enough, however, for me to understand some new things: All these men had been prisoners, but of what kind I was not sure. The captain himself had been in charge of them. It meant that somewhere during their voyage the captain had turned against his brother officers and had led these men into piracy. As for the prison ship's officers, I had little doubt what had been their fate.

Bit by bit, I was learning the history of Captain Grey.

CHAPTER TWELVE · *My twenty-first day: the view from Lookout Hill* ·

HAVING SPENT MANY HOURS in dutiful lessons, I requested of Jacob that I might see the workings of the lookout hill. He would not allow it until he had consulted with the captain, but the latter, seeing no harm, agreed that we could go the following morning, my twenty-first day of captivity.

We set out along the beach, around the bay where the sand was hard enough to travel at a brisk rate. After perhaps two miles, Jacob turned into the woods that came close to the water's edge. At first I could not see where he was leading me, for he entered into a thick underbrush, but quickly we came upon a beaten path that proved to be the regular way up toward the hilltop.

It was an easy enough climb at first, and the narrow path had few obstacles. Soon, however, we began a steep climb over and around rocks, but always on a way clearly marked. The higher we went, the greater the difficulty. The vegetation grew sparse until there was nothing but rock.

It must have taken an hour to climb to the top, which was a flat table of land. The view was worth our efforts. Below us the bay lay in perfect calm. The community, with its longboats on the beach, presented a picture of peaceful harmony. Beyond the bay, toward the interior, nothing was to be seen but endless forest.

Seaward was an even more breathtaking vista. The ocean was boundless, hedged only by the great circle of sky itself. Ships traveling these waters from any direction would be seen immediately. It would be easy to judge a ship's direction, purpose, even its strength, all to the advantage of the pirates. Once again I marveled at the captain's genius.

At the top of the hill, where we stood, was a small wooden shelter, the wood having been hauled up from below, for nothing one could call a tree grew there. It was no more than a protection for the man on duty. Each man took a turn on the hill, the schedule set by the captain. The man's job was to do naught but keep his eyes upon the sea. He would come up to the top at dusk, sleep on the hill, wake at dawn, and keep his watch until the next man came in the early evening. After sleeping one more night on the spot, the first man returned below.

The signal rockets lay in readiness, each one placed

upon a stick jammed in a cleft in the rock, pointed high. There were three of them: one was for the first alert, the other two signaled direction.

"What leads down from the seaward side of the cliff?" I asked.

"Nothing," Jacob replied. "And you'd best keep away, for it drops dead-off."

Curious nonetheless, I went as close to the edge as I dared, and despite my giddiness, lay upon my stomach and crawled forward until my head hung over the precipice.

It was indeed the sheerest of drops, with nothing but a mound of rubble at the foot of the cliff to break the fall. It was as if some portion of the hill had simply slid off into the sea. Unless one lay as I was doing, the man on the hill could not see the shoreline, or the island, only the sea.

As I watched, I observed sea gulls turning through the air. They had made their nests in various ledges upon the cliff. I saw other birds too: sparrows, swallows, and the like, darting here and there in great and graceful swoops.

Then I saw the pigeons.

Some were sitting on outcroppings on the face of the cliff itself. Others were circling around in the air. Since I had seen them nowhere else, I wondered whether my own pigeon was among them. It seemed a wild thought, but I could not help thinking that my pigeon traveled to this spot with my messages.

Looking over my shoulder and seeing Jacob and the

lookout in earnest conversation, I kept my eyes fixed below, watching the pigeons to see if they went to any particular place. In so doing I observed one pigeon make a series of circles, then dive toward the rock below and —disappear.

It happened so quickly I wasn't sure what it was I saw. Setting myself to waiting, my patience was rewarded when I spied another pigeon flying the same curious pattern. Then it too dived.

My eyes followed its flight. First it perched on a ledge close to the bottom of the cliff; the next instant, it too vanished. Without doubt it had gone into an opening in the cliff itself.

It was hard to believe, but what else was I to fancy other than the notion that my friend—the one who answered my message—was at the very foot of this hill!

I lay still, hoping I could determine with accuracy the whereabouts of the hole. Suddenly Jacob, with a pull at my toe, informed me that it was time to return. Reluctantly, but not wishing to give away my thoughts, I got up and followed him directly.

"It is a wonderful view," I said to Jacob as we walked along the beach toward the settlement.

"It is," he agreed.

"How did the captain find all this?" I asked. "Was it luck?"

"With him nothing is luck," he returned.

"You mean he knew this place before?"

"I suppose he did," he said, quickening his step.

"You don't like my asking questions, do you?"

"I can't say that I do."

"Why?"

"I'm here now," he said hotly, "better off than I can be elsewhere. And in time the captain shall lead us to an even better place."

So saying, he turned about, and keeping his distance between me and my questions, allowed for no more talk.

But that was not quite the end of my day. Benny greeted me at the door. "You'll be glad to know," he told me, "I've patched that hole in your roof." He touched his head in a mock salute. "Captain's orders."

CHAPTER THIRTEEN · *My second battle* ·

MORE THAN ANYTHING ELSE I wanted to get to the foot of the hill and do some exploring. I felt desperate about it now that I could no longer communicate through the bird. But not only was I in need of leave, I needed to go there alone. How I was to get permission to do that I had no idea. For though I was trusted more than before, I was never left entirely unattended.

As it turned out there was little enough time even for such thoughts. The next day, the twenty-second day since my capture, shortly after noon the rocket went up. A ship had been sighted.

Once again I was caught up in the host of men who hastened to the water's edge. This time, however, I was much more part of the action, for not only did I know what was about, I knew how to do some of it.

I suppose I could have sat down and refused to go. It remains on my conscience that I did not. The truth is, however, that the longer I was with the captain and his gang, the more I felt a part of it, so that despite my inner hatred I went along willingly. What else could I have done? I was very young and very much at the mercy of the captain.

Secure in the captain's boat, we hurried out of the bay, even as the second rocket spoke to tell us which way to turn. Acting accordingly, we rounded Sand Island and joined the sea.

Turning upon the ocean proper, the swells gathered us up and let us down with an easy sort of grace that in no way impeded our progress. The captain, sitting amidship, looked down the coast to spy the ship. All flowed to perfection, and I rather fancied he allowed himself a smile.

Under grey but calm skies, we pulled steadily. Jacob upon his great cannon raft, came smoothly in tow. It was the captain, as usual, who was the first to spy our prey.

"There she lies," he cried. "A schooner!" Then I heard him swear under his breath, glancing back toward the hill as if to ask a question. Nonetheless, he gave his commands quickly, sending, as usual, two of the boats deep to sea to outflank the oncoming ship, while the rest of us, the cannon raft included, came pushing up the middle.

It was a while before I could see the ship. She was much smaller than the one we had attacked before, and nothing so lofty in sail or great in bulk. But she was much faster.

The captain had a perplexed look on his face, for I think he was surprised to see something as small as the schooner marked as prey. Just as suddenly, he relaxed.

"A small one," he announced, loud enough for all to hear. "Short work and home."

The men, responding, leaned deeply into their oars, and we hurried over the waves.

Because both we and the schooner were moving so quickly, we closed with speed, so fast in fact that we were forced to hold back to make sure that the cannon raft was positioned properly. From all we could see, the schooner, flying right into our trap, had absolutely no suspicion of what lay ahead.

And so it may have been if an accident had not occurred. One of the men in the flanking boats had been in the process of priming his pistol when, inadvertently, he fired it.

The captain, instantly perceiving the danger, cried, "Have at her!" and the longboats pulled with all their strength.

On the raft, Jacob, though not yet properly positioned, uncovered his cannons.

The little schooner suddenly came alive. Men scurried everywhere on her decks, even up on her rigging.

Worse, four gunports swung open and cannons were run out.

Surprise—the captain's great advantage—had been lost. It was now we who were surprised. In fact, the schooner opened fire first, shooting at us indiscriminantly.

Jacob Small's cannon raft answered at once. Now it was the schooner's turn to be surprised, for its crew had been giving most of their attention to the smaller boats. Turning about, the schooner proceeded to direct her cannon shot at the raft, while sharpshooters perched on her rigging fired at the raft's crew.

Captain Grey began to shout out orders. In the main, they were to break off the fight and head for sea.

The schooner, however, was too quick for us, for she moved to the outside position to prevent any such escape. More than that, the fire directed against the raft had begun to take effect. The raft was slow and erratic in answering fire, but then it had never been built to fight in such a way. The strength of the operation lay in surprise—and that had been lost.

The captain now urged our own boat toward the raft. Reaching it, we leaped aboard—myself included—and rushed to man the guns. Jacob lay on the deck, his body rolling in death each time the raft was twisted by the waves.

Perhaps it was because I felt myself under fire. Perhaps one does not think at such moments. At any rate, I joined in as if comrades of mine were being unjustly attacked. Moreover, Jacob had taught me well; I was able to work close in hand with the men on the two working cannons, bringing up bags of powder as quickly as I could, and helping them load.

The stench of powder was everywhere. The smoke, the cries and shouts of the men, made everything twice as difficult. Under my feet the raft shook as if it were being held by a vibrating hand. Then the raft was struck by a ball. One corner gave way, and a second cannon was lost. Even as that happened we got off a shot—it had to be a lucky one—that seemed to return stroke for stroke.

The schooner, apparently hurt, swung about and broke off the fight. It was impossible to tell what damage we had done to her, for she turned and ran. We were safe, and we cheered accordingly.

But very quickly we saw why she had gone. The firing down, the smoke clearing, we looked about only to find ourselves alone on the sea. Only two longboats were still attached to the raft. The others had gone. The schooner, far from fleeing as we had thought, was merely giving chase to the other boats.

Four of our men lay dead on the raft. One cannon had been destroyed, another had gone over. With the unbalanced weight of the two remaining guns we listed badly.

Six men remained on the raft, the captain included. He called to the attached longboats to come up. They too had lost men to the schooner's sharpshooters, and others were wounded.

The captain, never saying a word about what had happened, placed those who were uninjured into the longboats, leaving the wounded on the raft. With even me manning an oar, we began to row home.

From time to time the captain stood, searching for some clue as to the others' fate. But they had either been scattered, sunk, or captured, for there was nothing to be seen of them.

Pulling as hard as we were able, with far less men than usual, we moved the unbalanced raft only with great difficulty. When darkness came, we dared not light any torches for fear that the schooner might still be lurking about.

The captain took his turn at the oars from time to time, but he was more upon the watch than anything else, looking for some hint of our companions as well as making certain of our direction.

The men with whom I labored said nothing at all. If they were angry or bitter about what had happened, they did not say so, at least not to me.

It was of course impossible to say whether the schooner had been looking for us or had merely found us. In any case, her deadly reaction, and her escape, meant that people would now take notice of us. One thing was perfectly clear: Captain Grey and his "nation" would no longer be hidden from the rest of the world.

CHAPTER FOURTEEN · *The twenty-third day* ·

I BELIEVE WE ROWED ALL NIGHT. I say "believe" because I am not certain; I was not awake for all of it. Perhaps the captain feared to go directly back to the bay. Perhaps he was lost. I know not. I only know that it was after dawn the following morning that we spied the tall rise of Lookout Hill.

This cheered us all, the more so as the sea was beginning to rise before a freshening wind.

Pulling harder than ever, the raft still in tow, we approached Sand Island. But as we tried to move behind it, toward the bay's entrance, we were confronted with a new problem: the tide was running *out*. This meant that a reduced and tired crew had to pull against the rushing waters. But there was no choice. With the captain himself at an oar, we stroked as hard as we could.

Once in the channel behind the island, the surging tide tried its utmost to keep us out. Our boats heaved and yawed, and the ropes attached to the raft seemed at every moment ready for splitting, so frayed had they become over the long hours.

The raft itself, caught in the swirling current, bobbed and tossed this way and that. It was hard to believe that we would be able to pull it in at all.

But pull we did. There was no other way. And bit by bit we gained, though as if our punishment had not been strong enough, the weather grew worse. The boats were manageable: it was the raft that was in constant danger.

The captain called upon us to pull and pull again. We did so, marking inches. The two boats, caught in the swirling, twirling narrowness of tide and channel were in constant danger of smashing into one another. Whatever strength we had left, we had to use it now. Where it came from I shall never know, but come it did, and we crept on our way.

Just as we began to see our way clear into the bay itself, when the tide was at its utmost, one of the ropes attached to the raft gave way. Instantly the raft began to spin, then was hauled back smartly by the one remaining rope, not however without a shock that proved to be too much for one of the guns. Its ropes could not hold, and the cannon careened into the water with a splash. This sudden loss meant that the raft became lighter, and we shot into the bay with such unexpected speed that it was difficult to look back and determine where the cannon sank.

We were, however, safe within the bay. Here the waters were calm.

The captain stood up; we too turned to look. Two more longboats had come in. That was all. Three had been lost or captured. Half of those who had gone out had not returned. Benny and Jacob had been killed. Of four cannons, only one remained.

The captain went straight to his house. I followed him. The other men went to their own huts. We were all exhausted.

It was a strange time. The community was in the greatest danger, a danger that far outweighed the sense of loss for the men who were gone. The question on all minds was: How long would it take before that ship came back? And how many others would she bring with her?

Yet nobody did a thing. Instead they waited upon Captain Grey, who had shut himself up in his rooms and did not appear. If there was any sense of rebellion among the men, that was the moment for it. I saw nothing. They were as dependent upon the captain's decisions as ever.

The morning following—my twenty-fourth—it rained all day. The day after was much the same, with strong, gusting winds and a cold dampness that numbed. Still, as long as the bad weather held, the men knew they were safe.

As for myself, with both Benny and Jacob gone, no one paid notice to me at all. Perhaps it was because I was with them in their desperate fight that they now assumed I was one of them. At first I felt that way myself. It took me time to perceive my new situation. With it came the understanding that I could, if I wanted to, explore the base of Lookout Hill.

I decided I had best leave no confusion as to my whereabouts. Accordingly, I went to the captain's door and knocked. There was no answer, so I knocked again.

"Who is there?" came his voice.

"Kevin."

It was a moment until I heard him say, "Come in."

I entered the dim room slowly. Such light as there was consisted of a single candle, which the captain had placed at the far end of the room. He himself, looking his worst, was in his great chair. I believe he had been that selfsame way from the moment he had returned. He was certainly wearing the same clothing, torn and spattered with blood as it was.

His face, ever long, seemed darker than ever. And his eyes, which lacked luster, seemed to see nothing but inner things, such pictures as I was glad I could not invent.

Shutting the door behind me, I stood before him. For a moment I was not sure he understood that I had actually come into the room, for he hardly took notice of me. A scraping motion with my foot on the floor reminded him that I was there.

"You saw what happened?" he said at last.

"Yes, sir," I replied.

"By now they have gotten word of our being here. They will be looking for us."

"Yes, sir," I repeated mechanically. It was all I could say.

"Were they looking for us?" he asked.

"I am sure I don't know," I managed to say, though not at all sure he was asking me the question.

He looked up at me. "It wasn't you—?"

"No, sir, I assure you. How could I?"

He waved his hand as if to say it didn't matter. Then he looked directly at me, and it seemed as if I saw some light in his eye for the first time. "Do you know what will happen if they come here?"

"No, sir, I don't."

"They will hang us all," he said, to which I replied nothing, though within I said, "Amen to that."

"Do you know who I am?" he asked me. "*Really* am?"

"Captain Grey," I answered.

"Yes, Captain Grey. Captain of what?"

"Of your nation, sir," I said, for I knew that was the way he fancied himself.

"What nation?" he said again. "What *other* nation?"

"I am sure I don't know."

"Nor do I," he said. He shut his eyes. "You did well yesterday," he said to me. "I was correct to trust you. What do you want?"

"I want to go out along the beach," I said.

"Is that why you came?" he said with a slight smile.

"Benny being dead—" I started to explain.

"I trust you now," interrupted the Captain. "You're one of us. You may do and go as you wish."

I waited for him to say something else, but he did not. As quietly as I could, I left his room and ran outside. After twenty-five days of captivity, I was beginning to feel free once more.

CHAPTER FIFTEEN · *The twenty-fifth day* ·

FEELING SECURE IN MY FREEDOM, I hurried down to the beach and set out along the shore, looking back once or twice to see if anybody was watching me. I saw no one.

When I got to the point where Jacob Small had indicated the path up to the hilltop began, I had to make up my mind which way to go. I did not want to go to the top, but I also did not want to be seen, as I feared I would be if I went along the bay.

Accordingly I went up the regular lookout path and followed it until it began to turn up the hill in earnest. There I left the path and began to push through the woods, for I had decided to approach the base of the hill from the seaward side. It was at the base that I had seen the pigeons.

It was not easy: I had to climb, push, and shove my way through, never altogether sure I was proceeding in the proper direction. I went along in this fashion for a long while when, through the trees, I spied a clearing, and heard the sea. Sure enough, in a short time I was looking out on the ocean coast, the high crest of the lookout hill to the left of me. I was exactly where I wanted to be.

Instead of going to the water's edge, I decided it would be most prudent to stay under the protection of the woodlands, just in case the person stationed on the top of the hill chanced to look down.

My task was not difficult. I simply circled around the base of the hill under the protection of trees, coming out at the sea-side bottom of the cliff. Once there, I was impeded by great mounds of rocks, boulders, even shifting sands. A good portion of the hill, battered by waves, had simply collapsed and slid to the bottom.

I managed to make my way, moving first up and then down, around, and even sometimes under the mass of grey, brown, and black rocks. Above me, gulls screamed at my intrusion, so much so that I wondered if they would give me away.

It must have been midday before I reached the front of the hill. Here I could all but see around to the entrance of the bay. Before me I observed the spit of land that was Sand Island, resting like a doorway to the bay.

The sea view, however, was not what interested me. Now that I had come to the spot I had most wanted to reach, I was unable to locate the place where I had seen the pigeon go.

There was nothing to do but sit as still as possible and watch. This I did. It had its first effect in calming the gulls. They stopped their squawking and circling to resume their normal business. This cleared the air, leaving me in a better position to see if any pigeons took to the sky. I sat motionless, my eyes searching.

Once or twice I did see pigeons, but they only circled and then sped off to sea. Or they went around to the other side of the cliff, where I could not observe them.

At last I was rewarded. One pigeon, directly above me, seemed to circle around and around in an unusual pattern. I rather fancied it was "my pigeon," but in truth they all rather look alike. Nonetheless, I followed closely, watching as its circles grew smaller and smaller. Then, right over my head—I even had to tilt my head back—I saw it land on a ledge some twenty feet above me. I must have blinked, for in the next instant I lost sight of it.

I kept staring at the spot, hoping that the bird would emerge again, but it did not. Deciding that it was as good as anything I might find, I proceeded to climb.

I never was a good climber, and trying to scramble up the face of the cliff was a particular kind of torture. I kept slipping back, skinning my knees and elbows.

Ascent seemed all but impossible. I was about to give up when I noticed a kind of ledge that gave the appearance of leading up toward the spot I wanted to reach. It was something of a retreat, but I was glad to try a new approach.

The ledge, when I reached it, was in places as much as two feet in width and served quite well as a path. As long as I kept the balance of my weight leaning toward the face of the cliff, I was in no danger of falling.

The ridge ran upward for some fifty feet upon a rather steep incline. I inched my way up slowly. Coming toward the top I moved with even greater caution, not wanting to frighten away any pigeons that might be there. Fortunately the ledge began to widen, so that I was able to turn about and even walk as if I were on a regular pathway.

Approaching the end of the path, I saw that it led to some kind of hole, or rock formation, I could not tell which. But as I came up to it, I found to my great joy that it actually was a hole, a hole quite large enough for me to enter.

Gathering what courage I had, and dropping down on my hands and knees, I moved into the hole. It proved to be something of a tunnel. Bird droppings assured me that it was, in any case, safe for birds.

Feeling my way—for it was darker the farther I went —I realized that the tunnel took a series of turns, first to the right, then down somewhat, then back again to the left. I pushed blindly on, and it was because I was going on so mechanically that when I turned the final bend, I almost cried out. There before me was a huge cavern.

I don't know what I expected, but my surprise could not have been greater. Stretched out in front of me was an area quite as big as the inside of a large room. I could not see all of it, for beams of light came through the walls in a number of places, giving a cloudy, misty quality to the air.

Parts of the walls were smooth, almost liquid to the look, oozing moisture and glistening in such light as there was. Other places were dull, dark, and dusty. The back reaches of the area disappeared into darkness so I could not in fact see how far it went. But as I grew accustomed to the dark, the cave seemed less large than I had first thought to be the case.

The air was filled with a curious, rustling sound of an almost ghostlike quality. It took me a few moments to reassure myself that it was nothing but birds, for indeed scores of birds had built nests all about the place.

Nonetheless, I hardly dared move from the entranceway, for my discovery of the cave had only added to my hopes that there might be someone there, the very person who had exchanged messages with me. My first glance, however, revealed no one in the gloom.

Uncertain what to do, I remained where I was, unmoving, merely looking about, gradually allowing my eyes to accustom themselves to the poor light. It was thus some time before I noticed a pile of black stuff upon the floor not far from where I had come in. It took a few seconds more to realize that it was the remains of a fire. That was all the evidence I needed to prove that someone was there—or had been there.

But where had that person come from, and how?

My mind went back to the ledge I had used to get into the cave. Crude as it was, it had seemed to be a path. Obviously it was just that, one beaten down by a human foot.

I moved forward a bit. Some of the birds stirred restlessly.

Cautiously, I rose to my full height and took a few steps toward the place where there had been a fire. I put my hand to the ashes, drawing it back with a start: I had touched a live coal. The fire had been used very recently.

I took some more steps forward, trying to look into the cave as far as possible, looking for some further evidence that might give me a clue to the person I sought. By mistake, my foot clattered against a rock. I stood motionless.

Ahead of me, in the far recesses of the cave, I heard an answering sound.

I crouched down instantly, listening and peering forward as hard as I could. Someone was at the farther end. Such was my excitement I could hardly breathe.

My first absurd thought was that it was a lion, or a bear, for coming out of the gloom toward me was a shaggy mane of hair with an indistinct face. Frightened, I stood up.

It was my sister's ghost!

CHAPTER SIXTEEN · *The twenty-fifth day continues ·*

I ROSE SLOWLY, soundlessly in my place, though if the beating of my heart could have been heard I would have put the loudest drummer to shame. I stood perhaps no longer than a few seconds, though it seemed forever to me.

The day we had been captured—less than a month before—I had heard my sister's screams. And I had seen her grave. Yet there before me, dressed in rags, hair as wild as any demon's, face scrubbed by hell's own hand, she seemed to stand.

Our eyes met. Her eyes, even as they grew large, were wild, strange, as befits one utterly lost.

I had always been taught that humans have souls but always believed such souls were no more than a vague sense of being. But since the time when I looked upon those strange eyes I can say that I do believe in souls, real souls, for I saw her's in her eyes. Surely, she saw mine.

I am old enough as I write this to claim a life of rich experience. I can say with the truth of years that the meeting of our eyes was the most extraordinary sensation of my life. It was so then. It remains so now. It proved to me that those eyes belonged to no spirit, no ghost.

"Cathleen?" I managed to say, not altogether willing to trust her name in any form save but a question.

No reply.

"Cathleen," I said again, my heart beating even more.

"Who are you," she spoke.

"It's Kevin, your brother."

"He's dead," she said, continuing to stare.

I shook my head no.

Whatever reservations, doubts, and fears remained simply fled away. Leaping toward one another, we rejoiced in an embrace that was both happiness and grief. What we had mutually suffered, lost, hoped, and could not hope were mingled in that embrace. When at length we could calm ourselves, we sat down facing one another, not for a moment wishing to remove the other from our eyes.

"I thought you were dead," we said at the selfsame time. And very quickly I told her what had happened when I had been captured, and how, after our father had been killed, I saw her run off, while I, being overpowered, heard shots and screams, and had then collapsed. I told her that when I had regained my senses she was nowhere to be seen. Since no one said anything to the contrary, I had believed she had been left dead in the forest. And, under the captain's orders, I had been marched to two graves, so that I gave up any hope whatsoever that she had been spared.

She in turn told me what she had done. Indeed she had fled, had been shot at, had screamed, had been pursued—but she *had* escaped. When, after hiding in fear for her life for two days, she made her way back to the spot where we had been surprised, she too found the two graves. Just as I, she knew one to be my father's. The second she had assumed to be mine.

It was easy to see what the captain had done: by making two grave mounds, he had made each of us believe in the other's death, depriving us both, in one stroke, of any hope of assistance from the other.

"I made my way to the coast," she continued to explain, "where I saw the settlement."

"But I was there!" I cried. "Did you not see me?"

"Perhaps I did," she said. "But I was so certain you had died that I would not even allow myself to have any hopes. I had to depend upon myself only. After all, there was no one dressed as you were."

I, of course, recollected the captain's cunning, remembering that he had me change my own clothes for the suit he had provided.

"At first," she continued, "I remained in the woods, for I was fearful of approaching anywhere near the settlement."

"But why did you not flee?" I protested, though naturally I was glad she had not done so.

"Where was I to go?" she countered. "I did not think I would be able to survive alone in the woods."

"You could have gone along the shore," I said.

"So I planned," she confessed, her eyes ever on me. "But my first thought was to keep alive, to find food and shelter. It was while looking for birds' eggs that I found this place. It was only a few days after we had been surprised."

"But then?" I asked.

"I received a message."

"From whom?" I cried.

"I don't know," she answered. "It was tied to a pigeon's leg, a pigeon that I noticed in the first place because of its tameness. All the message said was *Help me*. Believing you to be dead, I hardly considered that it had come from you, but I thought there was someone else in the settlement who had been captured, someone who might be of assistance to me."

"But it was I who wrote it!"

"You!" she cried, half laughing.

Then I told her all that I had done with the bird.

"Why did you not put your name to it?" she asked.

"I was afraid the captain would find it," I answered.

"The captain?" she asked.

"The one in charge of the camp."

"And I," she said, "was fearful that if the person found I was but a girl, he might not answer me at all."

We had, in fact, been talking to each other.

Then she asked me all about the captain, the settlement, and who was there and what they did. I told her as much as I could in the time we had.

"Why does he do these things?" she asked when I had done.

"He seems to hate everything," was my incomplete answer. "It makes no sense to me." Then I told her what had happened the last time we had gone out, and the captain's fears that the ship would be back.

"Do you think they will come back?" she asked.

"I don't know," I confessed. "But it is better, Cathleen, if we just go now," I pleaded. "We can make our way together."

"Perhaps we should," she said thoughtfully. "But maybe we should not. I can't tell you how many times, being here, how much I wanted to destroy them all."

"It's not possible," I objected. "There are too many."

"Don't you want to stop them?" she asked.

"I've wanted nothing else," I insisted.

"Then you have to go back to them," she said firmly.

"Why?" I protested. "If you can stay here without their knowing, why can't I?"

"If they let you come once, you can come again," she pointed out.

I sulked. I liked much more the idea of being free and staying here with Cathleen.

"What if that ship doesn't come back?" she said. "What if we can't get back to Philadelphia? We mustn't let them continue. You said they taught you how to fight with them. What sort of things?"

I told her some of the things, swimming lessons, using an oar, pistol loading, shooting the cannons. . . .

"Can you shoot off a cannon?" she suddenly stopped me.

"Not alone, I don't think. It needs at least two people. But this is foolish. We should leave now."

"What about the powder, the shot? Where is it kept?" she demanded.

"They have a small house for it, set off from the rest for safety's sake. But what good will it do?"

"Do you think you could get into that house?" she wanted to know.

"I suppose I might. Tell me what you're thinking."

Instead she stood up. "I'll show you."

Leading the way, she crawled out of the cave's tunnel. I followed. When we got to the entrance I was at first startled by the lateness of the day, for I had been unaware how much time had passed. It was already dusk. The sun, behind us, cast a great shadow over the water.

"Look over there," she said, pointing toward Sand Island.

I looked where she pointed but saw nothing, only the motion of the tide racing by the side of the island.

"Not at the water," she said. "At that low island."

I followed her arm. From where we were standing it did not look very different from before, a long, low stretch of sand with only a few rocks to break the line. Still I saw nothing unusual, until a sudden gleam caught my eye.

"You mean that bright thing?" I asked. The setting sunlight made whatever it was glimmer and spark.

"That's it."

The thing was partly up against the island beach, half in and half out of the water. "What is it?" I asked.

"A cannon," she replied. "It appeared there after the last storm."

I looked again. Cathleen was right. It was the muzzle end of a cannon, no doubt the one we had lost coming back from our disastrous attack.

"If we could get it out and clear," she suggested, "and if you could get shot and powder, and if we could work it—nothing at all would be able to come out of the bay."

CHAPTER SEVENTEEN · *Finding a way* ·

As SOON AS Cathleen explained her idea, I saw what would happen. A cannon aimed into the very mouth of the bay would prevent anything from coming out. Yet, as simple as Cathleen's notion was, it seemed impossible. The cannon was of no small weight. How would we be able even to move it, much less get it into position, without being seen?

Moreover, if we could do all that—and I saw no way we could—we then had to clean the bore, bring in shot and powder, and work the gun. After all, we were but two young people.

And even if we achieved all that? How many shots could we set off? Five? One? What would one shot be against the men that Captain Grey would hurl against us?

All this I told Cathleen, stressing with all my feeling the utter ruthlessness of Captain Grey. The more I told her, the more I felt opposed to the plan. Yet somehow my talk created in her just the opposite feeling. Perhaps it was her joy in our reunion, or her anger at what I had revealed. To all my objections she kept insisting that we must do as she explained. We needed only to find a way. In the end, despite all my reservations—indeed, my fears—I was prepared to be persuaded by my older, wiser, and dearly loved sister.

As it was, there was no time to solve the many problems. I had to return to the camp, if only to prevent anyone from becoming alarmed about my whereabouts.

We agreed that I would return to her as soon as possible, that in the meanwhile I would use such time as I had to search out possibilities of securing shot and powder.

Ready to part, I wished to hurry, not liking the idea of traveling alone through the dark woods. Cathleen, however, reassured me, insisting that we wait for total darkness. She herself never ventured forth when it was light. She knew the pathways well.

When it did become dark enough, she led me down along the ledge, then into the woods, until we came out on the far side of the hill, safely by the bay. We said our farewells hastily, and after mutual promises of care, I hurried home.

It was strange to return. I had not been missed, and no

one bothered to ask where I had been. They had all become used to me, considering me simply a good citizen in the captain's nation.

But inside my head the new knowledge, my new sense of self, my reunion with Cathleen, our plan for revenge, gave me an entirely different vision. I had the distinct feeling that I was once again a stranger. So one can well imagine my thoughts when I learned that during the day the captain had sent out word that we were to rebuild the floating battery, as well as refit the longboats.

This time, something different was to be done. This time, when they ventured forth the enemy ship was not to be sunk. Rather, it was to be captured. "It was time," the captain had announced, "to leave Freeman's Bay."

The men, who had hoarded their stolen goods for so long, could talk of nothing save such time when they would live as true aristocrats upon some distant shore. "The world is made of crooks," cried one with a wink, "poor thieves and rich gentlemen!"

The rebuilding of the raft, which began at once, was the first task. The remaining stock of good wood that had come from their original ship was enough to rebuild the battery according to their needs.

I was particularly interested in the means by which they hauled the wood to the shore, for it afforded me some time to observe the way great objects might be pulled into place. I, of course, was thinking of the cannon.

What I learned was this: it required a large number

of men, but with sufficient rope and good leverage, a remarkable weight could be shifted by a few. Would Cathleen and I be able to manage? I wondered.

The rebuilding of the floating battery went on, during which time I was unable to find time to escape to the hill and to Cathleen. I was not troubled by this, for I knew that she had been there alone for the better part of a month, and would be content. I was the restless one.

My chief worry was that the captain would discover that the sunken cannon had surfaced at the mouth of the bay. This proved an idle fear. Everybody in the camp was working on the land, and the lookout—I knew—had been carefully instructed not to announce any ships that might be passing. No warning rockets were to be fired unless a ship, say the schooner, came to attack us, as the captain feared was bound to happen sooner or later.

Since I knew that the men were making rapid progress on the raft, I realized that it would not be long before they had to try her out. Then, perhaps from the bay itself, they would notice the gun that had come up on the island.

As for the little house—where the shot and powder were kept—that was a different matter. I had gone into it before with indifference. Now, however, that I had designs on it, I felt as if my thoughts were a visible mark on my brow. I dared not go there alone. I was saved from my timidity by a request that I go into the place with one of the men: the captain wished to take inventory of all remaining stock.

I had no desire to take anything from the house itself, certainly not at that point, being much more concerned as to ways I might get things away on my own.

My job was to count off the large quantity of shot (mostly in round balls), powder, fuses, and the other various gun implements to my companion, who was preparing a list. As we began, an idea presented itself to me: I would call off *less* than was in fact there. Then, when I did take things, they would not be readily missed. In this fashion I managed to leave out of the count some ten balls, and as many bags of powder and fuses. If I could get them away, they would not have to be accounted for.

The next day being stormy—we were entering upon the storm season—I was again allowed to take my leave. Certain I was not watched, I ventured out to the cliff.

In the cave I found Cathleen in good spirits. I told her what was happening at the camp, as well as what I had done in regard to shot and shell.

Pleased, she made me come to the mouth of the cave. She pointed toward the spot where the cannon yet lay in the shallow water. It seemed to be farther out than I had remembered it. This observation, coupled with my report on the progress of the rebuilding of the raft, made us both feel that if we were to do anything, we had better attempt the enterprise sooner rather than later.

Indeed, the captain himself acted as though driven, the

more so since the season progressed with more bad days than good. Any day that proved suitable, we bent to the task of the raft. It was clear that the captain considered it most likely that the schooner would return and bottle him and his men in the bay. Haste was therefore safety. Sometimes I had the feeling that the captain actually knew what Cathleen and I hoped to do, and that it was a race to see who could do it first. That, however, I knew was impossible.

Such times as I had to myself I made lists within my head as to what we might need for the task that Cathleen and I were determined to do. Rope seemed to me what we needed first and most. I could think of no other way to raise the cannon from the water.

I managed to secure some rope and hide it in odd places. None of it was of fine quality, and I could find only bits and pieces, some of them no longer than a foot in length. But bit by bit I managed to secure a goodly length.

In the short space of time I had to leave the settlement, there were moments enough to run out for brief meetings with Cathleen. We seemed to talk about little else but our hopes. Sometimes I thought this was so because we really knew that our enterprise had only a faint chance of success.

But one day Cathleen met me with a cry of "I've found a way!"

Eager to hear any idea, I urged her to explain.

"I've been watching the cannon," she began. "And when the waves and tide are high, it seems to rock a bit. If we could hold it every time it moved, and not let it slip back, perhaps the waves would push it up on the shore. We'd only need to secure it to the rope, then take up the rope bit by bit."

"But that would require our being on the island for a long time," I protested. "We would be seen."

This she agreed was the real danger, but it being the only idea we had, and since the floating battery was all but rebuilt, we decided we had to go on.

From that moment, all my efforts were bent on getting more and more pieces of rope to Cathleen. She, in turn, spent her days securely binding the small bits together. It was slow work, as she kept insisting that it had to be perfect. For once, she was thankful she had spent time in a millinery shop. With a week's constant effort, she made the rope as long and as strong as was possible.

We decided that the next thing we had to do was swim out to Sand Island and try to fix the rope around the cannon. Again I warned her about the strong tidewaters at the mouth of the bay and in the channel. Her reply was that we would swim at slack tide, that pause between the turning of the tides. As it was, each day slack tide came later and later in the afternoon. Within days, it would come at dusk.

We agreed, therefore, that at the very next opportunity I would join Cathleen, and we would attempt to swim to the island with the rope.

The next two days at the captain's "nation" were agony for me. The captain, in a final burst of energy, swore before all that he would have the floating battery completed. The men agreed, for there was a general belief among them that a major storm was approaching. Once the storm had passed, the likelihood of ships appearing off the coast would be greatly heightened.

Sure enough, within those two days, whatever blueness was in the sky was sucked up in an enveloping grey. The wind shifted, and all noted that the storm was fast approaching. One man, after studying the birds and clouds, announced that it was to be no less than the first hurricane of the season.

That meant little to me. As far as I was concerned, a storm meant only that I would be free. Freedom meant that I could go to Cathleen.

I did go late that afternoon. By the time I reached her, the wind had begun to whip the tops of trees. From the mouth of the cave I could see a spray of ocean bursting over the seaward side of Sand Island higher than I had ever seen before.

On the ledge of the cliff, we waited. As it grew darker, our eyes were focused on the cannon. In the rising thrust of the waves, it rocked back and forth like the pendulum of a clock.

We were determined to proceed.

CHAPTER EIGHTEEN · *The storm* ·

WE WAITED PATIENTLY, though never did the dusk descend more slowly. We had to choose *the* moment, the time when there would be the least chance of our being seen yet still be able to see for ourselves. Moreover, we had to observe the tide. Too soon or too late would be equally fatal. As we waited, the waters, pushed by an increasing wind, rose and fell at an alarming rate.

"One of the men said it would be a hurricane," I informed Cathleen.

She said nothing at first, but after some thought replied, "The stronger the waves, the easier it will be to move the cannon."

And indeed the cannon was swaying more than it had before. If we did not act soon, we might lose it altogether.

Nonetheless, we remained on the ledge for another hour until, by unspoken agreement, we decided it was dark enough to make the attempt. The tide seemed right, if not perfect. Hauling our rope along with us, we moved down to the water's edge.

We had decided that once we went out from the safety of the cliff, we would rush into the water without hesitation. This we tried to do, scrambling down the face of the cliff, half jumping, half slipping. At the bottom we each took one end of the rope—it was no more than thirty feet in length—and tied it around our waists.

I know I speak for both of us when I own that we offered up as fervent prayers as was possible, for the difficulty of our task came upon us as it never had before. Though the tide seemed still, the water was wilder, the effect of the constantly rising wind. The channel itself was no more than a hundred feet across, save for the tide, not a difficult swim. But the churning waters, merged with the darkening sky, blended into a gulf of immeasurable distance.

Our prayers sent forth, our rope checked and re-checked, we stepped into the water. In spite of ourselves we paused knee deep, the shock of the coldness numbing our desire. Then, as was always the case,

Cathleen plunged boldly into the waves. I followed.

Cathleen remained ahead of me. Dreading that I might hold her back and thus pull her under, I fought against the water the moment I hit it, my sense of fear overwhelming. The waves, now that I was in them, were on me again and again, spinning me as if I were on a spit.

No sooner had the first shock worn off when I felt myself sucked down by undercurrents. The tide had begun to turn. I took mouths of water, gagged, spat out, found voice enough to cry for help.

If ever the goodness of God manifested itself to me, it was at that moment. I became acutely conscious of the rope tugging at me, a tugging that called my mind back to what I needed to do—to swim—which I had yet to do. Desperately, I flung out my arms and in such wild fashion began to move.

Very quickly I lost all sense of direction. The darkness, the foam, and the high waves enveloped me, lifted me, dropped me. The upper half of my body, pulled by flailing arms, went one way; my feet, dragged into the undertow, went another way.

It was the rope that saved my life. It pulled at me, gave weight and direction, so that somehow, I had the sense to follow its line. The one thing I sought more than anything else, more than land itself, was Cathleen. She was, I knew, ahead of me. With blind desire, I pushed on. Somehow I assumed she had reached land. I had to reach it with her, or drown.

So I swam.

The water roared about me, in me, over me. I felt the

coldness, not the wet. My body seemed separate from my mind. My arms and legs moved on their own. I tried to wipe my face of water, only to be washed again. I tried to stand. I sank. I climbed a liquid ladder to the air. I had the sensation that the rope was pulling at me. I let myself be pulled, shoving the sucking waters away as I would push through a thicket of thorns.

Suddenly my foot struck something solid. I reached to grab it, and my head went underwater. I choked, burst up, and then collapsed, groping for the soft and shifting sand with my fingertips. I could not, would not, get a firm hold. Losing breath, I began to slip back. I felt a hand about my arms, and Cathleen pulled me to the shore.

I stood, shaking, the water all about me. The storm was no longer wind and waves; now the rains had come. I had gone from a watery sea to a wetter land.

"Where are we?" I cried to Cathleen, who was still holding me up.

She couldn't hear me. The sounds of the storm made normal speech impossible.

"Where are we?" I screamed.

"On the island," she shouted into my ear, all the while pushing me farther up the shore.

We climbed higher on the land without any true sense of direction, the darkness preventing us from seeing where we were. Lightning revealed only that we were on the island, nothing more. What it chiefly showed us was that there was no place to hide. The sand, stone, and rocks left us unprotected against the storm. Another flash of lightning—they came quicker now, as did the thunder—provided enough illumination for us to discover a large rock not far from where we stood. Clinging to one another we made our way to it, kneeling by its side, opposite the wind. Even that protection, and it was scant, was something akin to comfort, short comfort at that. While it could hardly become more dark, it was becoming colder.

"Can you walk by yourself?" Cathleen called.

"I believe so," I replied, glad to be able to sit somewhere.

"We have to find the cannon," she cried.

"We can never do it," I answered.

"Stay here then," she said to me, refusing to listen. "I'll come back when I find it."

Miserable as I was, I would not be left alone. I got up quickly, and though she repeated that she would return, I insisted on following.

It was a strange sort of journey. For each forward step we took, the wind tried to throw us back two steps, the sand and rain doing every bit as much. Though the island was not large, it seemed immense, and with the sea running high I was sure we would miss the cannon, if we had not already done so.

But find it we did. Its muzzle pointing down, it lay upon its wooden carriage. This carriage, still intact and only half submerged, was like a sled resting on the sand. The entire cannon was much farther out of the water than it had appeared from the other side of the channel. Under the constant beating of the water, it rolled up and down steadily.

Finding the cannon brought back much of our energy. The storm, difficult as it had been for us, suddenly seemed of small concern. What we had come for, the moving of the cannon, was the only thing we desired.

But our pleasure quickly sank beneath the problem of how next to proceed. Indeed, we stood there momentarily, doing nothing, until Cathleen brought us back to our original plan.

We had kept the rope around us, as much for safety's sake as for anything else. This rope Cathleen now untied. Then, telling me to remain in one spot, she waded back into the surf by the cannon's side. She had to move with great caution, feeling her way, ever fearful of being struck by the rocking gun.

"Kevin!" I heard her cry. "There's rope already here!"

I hurried to her side. She grabbed my hand, and thrust it down into the foaming waters. Sure enough, there was rope. It was, I realized, the rope that had held the cannon to the raft. It had severed, but it had not come undone from the cannon. A great stroke of luck.

"How long is it?" I shouted into her ear.

She slid her hand along the slippery rope. It proved to be long enough for me to stand high upon the shore and then some. Jacob Small had not been sparse.

"It must be on the other side too," I cried at her.

Quickly Cathleen went around, ducked down, and

came up with an even greater length of rope. She pulled it up and waded back to shore.

Then, calling to me, she tied these rope ends around us, and we both moved up the island as far from the cannon as was possible, so that the rope, tied to us and tied to the cannon, held tightly. As the rope grew taut, I could feel the cannon as if it were something live. The beating waves, lifting the machine up and down, caused a movement that ran along the rope and into us.

"Pull back against the rope!" Cathleen shouted to me. "Lean against it. Let the cannon come to us. Try not to let it slip back!"

At her command I pushed my heels into the sand and simply leaned back against the rope.

We tried to keep the lines tight, hoping that we were right, that the gun, lifted by the waves, would ride up on the sand. Here again, fortune favored us. If the cannon had not been on its sledlike carriage, it hardly could have moved. But the carriage slid upon the sand and did not sink.

In all honesty, I don't know what we really did. We stood there, out beneath a whirling storm that, if anything, seemed to blow worse. Many a time I slipped and fell. Sometimes we called to one another. But always the tug from the cannon recalled us to our task.

How long we stood that way I shall never know, for standing and then eventually falling, I succumbed to exhausted sleep.

CHAPTER NINETEEN · *The white morning* ·

WHEN I AWOKE my first thought was that it was still raining. In fact, the thick air was only the white wet mist of very early dawn. I sat up and tried to look about. Cathleen was a few feet from me, still asleep. In front of me, the sea heaved high, like an exhausted runner. I could not see across the channel or into the bay, though I knew from the whiteness of the air that it was day.

The last thing I sought was the cannon. I looked down at the rope that was still about my waist and followed it, like a lengthy fuse, toward the water's edge. I saw nothing. The line ran into a great pile of sand and seaweed that had been thrown up by the storm.

Feeling ill, I turned away, not willing to look on our

failure. Instead, I plucked at the knotted rope around me, thick with weeds, sand, and water, difficult to pull apart.

After I had freed myself, I crawled over to where Cathleen lay. Reluctant as I was to wake her, I knew we had to get off the island as quickly as we could. I shook her shoulder.

She woke slowly, her face patched with sand. Recollecting where she was, she sat up abruptly and turned at once to where the cannon should have been.

"It doesn't matter," I said by way of comfort. "I won't go back to the settlement again. We'll go back to your cave. And when we're rested we'll just go through the woods and try to find our way home."

Cathleen paid no attention to me. Instead, she crawled toward the mound of sand and with her hands began to scoop away the pile. I had no idea what she was doing.

Then I saw. Beneath the pile was the cannon. It *had* come up. Not completely. Part of the carriage was still in the water, But it had come high enough. The muzzle and the trunnion—the body of the piece—were free of the sea. And while it was not aimed with great accuracy, it *was* pointing into the mouth of the bay. Even if they should pass north, we could manage at least a shot or two.

"Let's clear it all!" I cried, diving at it and beginning to scratch at it like a dog digging for a bone. Cathleen caught me and held me back.

"Leave it!" she cried. "It's perfectly hidden in the sand. I don't think they'll be able to see it at all."

She was right. Not only had it come up, but it was also hidden from view. We needed only to scoop out the bore, and clear the touchhole to have it ready.

We were so elated by what had happened that we were quite brought back to life. We needed that, too, for we had to swim back across the channel, and as yet we could not even see across to the cliff.

What we did was to go to the southernmost point of the island. Happily, the tide was churning in. Then, still tied together by our own rope, we waded in. This time we let the water carry us, making sure only to keep our heads above water and edge closer and closer to the cliff. In moments we were on the rocky land beneath the cave.

In the meantime the fog, though no lighter, was yet more bright. Behind us, the island was all but lost to our sight. The hill above disappeared into the mists.

We were both excited, but the urgency we felt forced us to give way to the realities of our new situation. While it was true that the cannon had been shifted and placed in a way to be used, its aim, at best, meant that we would have but two shots. Certainly we would not have more. On these shots alone all our fortunes sat. Once we began to shoot, we would be discovered and open to attack. We either had to stop the captain then, and completely, or forfeit our lives for nothing.

In the interim I had to return to the settlement. There was already much risk in my having been gone so long. Fortunately it was still early in the morning, but the white fog was growing whiter, a sure sign of a rising sun. The mist might lift at any time. I had to hurry. We agreed that at every safe opportunity I would steal away, taking as much as I could carry.

It was left to me to decide when I could come, the chief concern being that it be done secretly. It would take a number of trips. It was also agreed that as I brought in the supplies, Cathleen would take them out to the island herself, piece by piece. When she would do this, at dusk or dawn, she would decide.

The first thing I had to bring was canvas. She would put this over the cannon, then heap sand over it. Thus the cannon could be kept in as fixed a state of dry readiness as was possible.

Having agreed to all of this we parted, for the first time with a clear sense that we would at least *have* our chance, which was far more than I, for one, considered possible a few hours before.

I set off at once for the settlement.

Since I was in a hurry and felt protected by the fog, I did not go my usual way through the woods. Rather, I went round the base of the cliff, directly to the beach that edged the bay. This I managed with ease. Once I reached the sand I ran easily, trusting to my senses, for I could still see little. Indeed, even as I ran, I looked back. The mouth of the bay was simply not to be seen. Ahead, I saw no more. I was glad of it: the last thing I wanted was to be observed.

I ran on, using the lap of the water on the beach to guide me, trusting to my sense of place to lead me. Then I stopped suddenly, for I heard a sound. I listened hard, and the sound came again. Someone was treading the sand.

I remained motionless, but all my calmness drained away. I heard another sound, closer. I turned, and in turning, became confused, knowing not which way to go. There was nothing but the whitened air, which, growing in brilliance, dazzled me. I could have cried out in vexation! After all that had happened I was lost! I dared not move.

Then I heard a click. I recognized it instantly as the sound of a pistol being cocked.

I saw, even at that moment, the shadow of a form. I panicked, ran, crashed into someone, and spun head-long into the sand. I felt a hand on my neck. Twisting around, I looked up. It was the captain, one hand gripping me, the other holding a pistol not a foot from my face.

CHAPTER TWENTY · *The captain's story* ·

THE CAPTAIN, unmoving, stared at me for some time before he spoke.

"Where have you been?" he asked.

I couldn't speak.

"Where have you been?" he repeated, louder.

"I was out looking for birds' eggs," I managed to lie. "And when the storm came last night I was afraid to come back and stayed in the woods."

"You were missed," he said.

"I am sorry."

"I thought you might be gone."

"Not I!"

He must have believed me, for he released his grip and bid me stand.

After studying me, he turned to look toward the bay. The mist had begun to dissolve beneath the sun. We could just make out the floating battery on the bay.

"The battery is finished," he said after the longest time. "The next ship that passes we must take. We shall have to leave this place before the next storm comes."

"Where will you go?" I asked, my voice returning with the sense that I was not undone.

"Where will *we* go?" he returned, with something of a smile. "There are places enough in Spanish America. And from there . . ."

He did not complete his thoughts, but instead returned to his present concern. "We need all the men we have in the longboats to tow the raft. When the rocket goes up, you are to be by the guns, tending the powder box. You'll serve under Richard Johnson. He saw you at your tasks before and will be pleased to have you."

"I don't wish to go!" I blurted out.

"Why not?" he asked.

I was angry at myself for having said anything, but it was too late.

"Why not?" he repeated.

"I don't believe I'll do well," I replied.

"I assure you, you will do well enough," said the captain. He looked hard at me. "Or do you fear that we will fail? Or is it that you wish us to fail?"

I said nothing.

"We must not fail," he said.

I got up, and the mist no longer hiding the way, I started to trudge toward the house. I had no wish to argue the point or say anything that might reveal my thoughts.

"Wait!" he called.

I turned.

"It is time you learned why all this is necessary," he said. "Do you wish to know?"

I was torn by my desire to know and my equal desire to get away from him as quickly as possible.

"Go to my room and wait for me," he ordered. "It's time you knew."

Reluctantly, I went as he bid, glad at least to stand before the fire in his room, which warmed me considerably. At length he appeared, made a point of shutting his door, took a seat, and sat back and looked at me closely.

"I was English born," he said softly, "but like a slave was shipped when a boy to America for what others called a crime, the stealing of a trinket. Set free, I became an American, as good as any other. And quick enough to come to the defense of my country's aid when her liberties were threatened by the British.

"I joined early, in 1775. A patriot of liberty," he said scornfully. "And where, sir, where, in defense of liberty, was I sent?"

"I don't know."

"To fight Lord Dunmore's Ethiopian Regiment!" he fairly screamed. "Do you know who, and *what*, that was?"

I shook my head no.

"Black men! Slaves. Yes, slaves given their freedom

if they fought for the British. I fought those black men and helped to beat them. I made them slaves again. A noble stroke for liberty, was it not?"

I said nothing.

"But more!" he said, suddenly shouting, as his anger began to build. "I fought with great Washington, and very fine he may have been, a slave of his own by his side, while the Philadelphia politicians grew fat with their contracts and their deals. Liberty, sir, liberty for what!"

He continued in a quieter tone. "I offered to join the British. Not for coin. Not for reward. For honor! I went to them secretly, and they accepted me. And where did they send me to fight?"

Again I shook my head.

"Against my Connecticut, with Benedict Arnold's American Legion. Against New London town. Against my own family who resided there. But I learned of this plan, and all honor, I sent word to my family, to my wife and child. A young man, like you."

"Then they escaped!" I said.

"They did not," said Captain Grey steadily. "The British intercepted my message. It never reached my home. Not that I knew that. They told me nothing. It would interfere with their strategy.

"Thinking they were safe I led that attack. My family was destroyed. Both of them. My wife and child. When I learned what I had done I fled again. Twice a traitor! Back to the American side with a hatred of the British that had no equal in the land.

"No task was hard enough for me. Whether in the West, or scouting on these shores where I found this place. I stayed with the Americans until the war was won. Then I was given a last command. How I welcomed it! To take a ship of captured British soldiers—prisoners—back to England. I was captain of the prison ship!

"Some of the men I had fought against, some I had fought with. And what did I learn about these soldiers whom I hated so? They were British citizens to the man, and not one, *not one* had come to fight willingly. Each of them had been taken against his will to fight a war he did not want. Weren't these men also slaves?

"I set them free. And brought them here.

"Where's the freedom on this earth?" asked the captain. "Who fought for liberty? Who won it? Who lost it? All the men I've ever seen are slaves to other men, to governments or such. The only man who's truly free is the one who is part of nothing, and wars against the rest of the world.

"If my son were alive, I'd teach him that. That's why I let you be. You are to be my son and act for me.

"I'll educate you," he said. "Teach you to fight for the slaves of the world. You'll set them free. Yes, you'll come with me. I don't intend to let you go. Ever."

He sat back in his chair, exhausted by his outburst. "Remember," he concluded, "you're to be on the floating battery." He turned away. "It's the safest place. We must have a ship."

Dismissed, I hurried out of his room.

CHAPTER TWENTY-ONE · *The rocket goes up* ·

THE STORM HAVING PASSED, we came in for a time of good weather. Though September, it was all but spring again. The air hung light and clear and blue, the breezes almost balmy. All that remained to do for the battery was to outfit it with new cannons. This proved to be no problem. Extra cannons, from the captain's original ship, had been kept for just such an emergency behind the powder house. I helped drag the guns to the shore, thus having the curious distinction of setting up the guns on both sides of the battle lines.

In the middle of the bay the repaired raft, fitted again for battle, with four cannons on the ready, floated at her ease. The waiting longboats, fewer in number than before, reposed upon the beach. So, too, *our* cannon, hidden by the sands upon the island, also waited.

The men of the camp alternated between talking of their future and packing their stolen stuff. Some bartered, sold, or exchanged what they had. The goods that had belonged to those who had perished in the battle with the schooner were divided among the thirty-odd remaining with amazing good grace. All was made ready for the capture of a ship and then departure.

There were times when I wanted no more than to leave this place, joining with Cathleen to make our way back to civilization.

But she would not hear of it, insisting that we must stop the captain. Even when I told her what I had learned about him, the story of his past, she would not change her mind.

"He is a traitor to everything," she insisted. "He blames all but himself for what he himself has done."

"He wanted me to be his son," I said, feeling guilty at the thought.

"You already had a father," she reminded me, "and he was also mad."

There was nothing I could say to that.

I spent my energies in moving the small store of shot and powder, a rammer as well as fuses, from the powder house to the cave. I could not go every day, though I would have gone twice a day if it had been possible. But I could hardly allow myself to be seen carrying loads of things. And though we had decided upon a possible maximum of two shots, we thought it best to have more. I had to make many trips.

Each time I brought the things—beginning with the canvas cover for the gun—Cathleen swam out to the island and hid them safely by the cannon, making sure they would not get wet. There was no great difficulty in this, except for the powder. It mattered not that other things got wet; the powder had to be absolutely dry.

The way Cathleen managed this was most clever. In the cave were, as I have said, numbers of birds with their nests. Cathleen had used their eggs for food. Now she gathered some of these eggs, and pricking a small hole at one end, sucked out the meat. Then she let the eggs dry. Once dry, she filtered the powder into the egg-shells with her fingers, grain by grain. A touch of wood pitch—which I collected as I came through the woods—and her "eggs" were sealed. She even brought over live coals in this manner, to keep a spark at hand.

In short time all was ready at the cannon.

And so we made our final plans: When the rocket went up, she was to swim at once to the island and go to the cannon, which had been loaded in readiness for the first shot. That she could do alone.

While that was happening I was to run around the beach along the inside of the bay. Once at the mouth of the bay, I would swim the channel and join her.

Since we were certain that I could be there in good time, she was not to shoot until I joined her, after which the two of us could quickly load the cannon a second time and attack the floating battery as it swept by.

Such was our plan.

It did not happen that way. A few days after making these plans, with only enough powder for three shots on the island, the rocket did in fact go up.

It was early morning, not far past dawn. I was sleeping when I was brought to quick life by the sound of the rocket's dull thud. There was no mistaking that sound. Below where I slept, I could hear the captain's shouts and the calls from the other men already racing toward the beach.

I sprang up, my head still unclear, trying to decide what to do. I never got the time to think up a plan.

At the foot of my steps, the captain cried: "Hurry, boy! To the raft. To the raft!"

I jumped up and ran down the steps determined to bull my way past him and rush along the beach as we had planned. But once below, the captain completely blocked my way.

"Out with you!" he yelled.

Pushing me before him, but never letting me go, we hurried out the door. As soon as we got outside, I tried to bolt, but as if he were expecting it, he held me with so strong a grip that I called out in pain.

"Into the boats!" he roared. Still holding me, he shoved me in the direction of the shore, where the men were already waiting.

I had no choice. With the captain over me, I all but

fell into a boat, and the boat once filled, we pushed away.

We headed for the raft with long, even strokes. I looked wildly about, trying to find a way out, but could not make a move. As we came against the raft, the captain picked me up and fairly flung me on board. In past times he had kept to one of the longboats. This time he joined me on the battery with the other men.

The raft crew on board, the other boats, four in number, began to pull on the raft even as we threw off the anchor. I looked to see how quick the tide was running out. It was going very fast.

The raft began to move. I turned to the island but could see nothing; I had no idea if Cathleen had even reached it.

I stood for a moment, trying to decide what to do, when a shout from the captain brought me back to my senses, and I began to do my work, to open the powder box in the middle of the raft and get the charges ready.

The raft was slipping smoothly toward the mouth of the bay. Faster and faster we went. The captain, from his position on the floating battery, urged the men in the boats to pull harder with every oath he could command. The men, responding to his urgent voice, pulled at a furious pace.

I kept looking toward the island, trying to see some sign of Cathleen. I still had not seen her but decided I must find a way to tell her where I was, so that she did not shoot. Without me, she could get off only one shot, and one shot would never be enough.

The second signal rocket went off, telling us which

way we were to turn out of the bay. The signal indicated that we would cross right in front of the hidden cannon.

Closer and closer to the mouth of the bay we swept, much faster than I had anticipated. Then I saw Cathleen's head bobbing in the water, swimming quickly toward the island. In spite of myself, I cried out, "Cathleen!"

The captain turned about. "Who are you calling?" he demanded.

I only shook my head, and he, confused, looked from me back to the water without yet spying her. But I could see her struggling against the tide, trying to reach the land.

We were only sixty yards from the mouth of the bay, now firmly caught in the tide and rushing faster and faster, when I heard a shout. One of the men in the forward boats had stood up and was pointing. Cathleen, having reached the island, was now in plain view, rushing toward where the cannon lay.

"Who is that?" bellowed the captain.

We were now thirty yards from the island. Cathleen, having reached the site, wildly began to throw off the canvas from the cannon. In an instant, the low sun flashed against the gun's bright muzzle.

"Cannon!" came the shout from forward.

The captain, who had been straining to see, suddenly turned and made a grab for me.

Recoiling, I spun about and in desperation jumped headlong into the water.

I hit the water hard, but fearful of being crushed by the floating battery, I let myself sink as deep as I could, all the time pushing toward what I believed would be the island. I felt myself being swept by the tides, up and out. Like to burst, I pushed upward, kicking and clawing at the water. My head broke the surface only twenty feet from the island. Even then, I was moving rapidly toward it.

I saw Cathleen standing by the cannon. "Cathleen!" I shouted, and began to swim frantically.

She turned, saw me, then turned back. I heard a crash. She had fired off the first shot.

The cannon worked perfectly. The ball, aimed low, fell short of the first of the longboats just coming into the channel. But the shot was good enough to send up a great spray, swamping the boat and causing it to flounder.

Reaching the island, I began to run toward Cathleen, who was already swabbing out the muzzle. Looking back, I saw the raft begin to swing in an erratic fashion. The loss of one boat brought confusion on the others, causing the lines to go slack. The raft, under no control, began to twist slowly.

As I came up to Cathleen she was dumping in the bag of powder. Instantly I grabbed the rammer and stuffed the powder down the muzzle while she picked up a ball.

When I pulled out the rammer, she let the ball roll down, even as I jumped toward the cannon's touchhole, trying, with trembling fingers, to pour powder down. Cathleen, hardly waiting, stuffed down the fuse. The gun was set. Only then did we turn around to see what was happening.

All the boats were out of control. The captain, standing on the raft, called and shouted but could do nothing. Vainly the men tried to reorganize, only to have their oars become entangled in the lines. The floating battery, swept by the current, spun out like a broken top, crashing into the boats.

Cathleen touched the fuse with a spark. Again the cannon fired; it lurched over, but only after releasing the ball.

The distance was short. The ball flew straight, crashing into the powder box in the center of the raft. There was a huge explosion.

"This way!" cried Cathleen.

She pulled at me and together we started to run toward the opposite end of the island, certain that we would be pursued.

Midway we turned and stopped. There was no one following us. The floating battery was nowhere to be seen. But off in the distance we saw sails, the intended victim.

"Look there!" I cried.

The schooner had returned at last. The captain had been right.

CHAPTER TWENTY-TWO · *The end of the affair* ·

WE HAD DONE what we set out to do. How many men drowned, we never knew for sure. The raft was completely destroyed, the longboats sunk or broken. The only bodies recovered were those of lifeless men.

The schooner, dropping anchor off the island, sent in boats of armed men. All they found were Cathleen and myself. Their amazement knew no bounds.

I took them to the settlement, where all the stolen goods were recovered. The town, Captain Grey's "free nation," was systematically destroyed by flame. On the shore I found his pure white flag, discolored by a stain of blood.

Cathleen and I were taken on board the schooner, there to tell all that had happened to us. When we had done, considerable praise was bestowed upon us.

We set sail and in a fortnight's time rejoined our mother's cousin, good Mrs. Barry. We took up our lives as we had lived before, poor relations to an excellent Philadelphia businesswoman.

Sometimes, at night when I can't sleep, my mind recalls that time. I think of all that happened, but most of all I think of Captain Grey.

When the bodies on the shore were counted, I had been asked to point him out. I pretended to do so, but the man I pointed to was not in fact the captain. I alone knew that his body was not there.

He was wrong. I know he was wrong. He could not be right, no more than my poor father was. Yet, in spite of myself, recollecting that I was never positive of his fate, while I cannot wish him well, I wish him a life to live.

I think, knowing him as I do, to live would be his greatest pain. For myself, I had enough of death for one so young.

May God have mercy on Captain Grey's soul. Amen.

Avi's many books for young readers include the Newbery Honor books NOTHING BUT THE TRUTH and THE TRUE CONFESSIONS OF CHARLOTTE DOYLE. His other popular works include the *Tales from Dimwood Forest* series, NIGHT JOURNEYS, and ENCOUNTER AT EASTON, as well as tales of mystery, fantasy, and historical fiction. You can visit Avi's website at **www.avi-writer.com**